Livermore Wine Country Literary Harvest

2008

An anthology of works by writers who come to read and listen at

4th Street Studio's

Saturday Salons

edited by

Karen L. Hogan and Selene Steese

WingSpan
PRESS

All materials in this publication remain copyrighted by the respective authors. No part of this book may be reproduced in any manner whatsoever without written permission except in the case of brief quotations embodied in critical articles or reviews.
For information, address WingSpan Press, P.O. Box 2085
Livermore, CA 94551.

Cover and Interior Design: Karen L. Hogan

ISBN: 978-1-59594-198-5

Dedicated to

William Faulkner

—because he told us to banish fear from our workshop so we could write about the problems of the human heart in conflict with itself

&

Kurt Vonnegut

—because he told us to find our own voice

The weight of this sad time we must obey;
Speak what we feel, not what we ought to say.

from King Lear
Act V, Scene III
by William Shakespeare

Table of Contents

Foreword ix
by Rachael Lavezzo-Snedecor

A Story is Meant to be Passed Around 1
by Karen L. Hogan

Why I Write, Part I 8
by Selene Steese

The Best Sports Play I Ever Saw Involved a Trombone 10
by David Collins

Too Long Between Nothing and Something 12
by Timothy B. Rien

The Day the Ice Cream Disappeared 21
by Susan Mayall

Midnight in Texas 24
by Bryant Hoex

Halloween Hair 37
by Cynthia Patton

ego at large (again!) 43
by sandra kay

Sweet Man 44
by Tom Darter

Whitcomb's Trill 46
by J.D. Blair

(untitled) 49
by Ian Ray Armknecht

NanoNonFiction 50
by Jason Hambrecht

Genre Nano-Fiction 51
by Tom Darter

Not Really Kafka, Just Kafka-esque 52
by David Hardiman

Puberty Problems 59
by Frank Thornburgh

Comin' Down the Hill 61
by Ethel Mays

The Cow and the Mountain Lion 63
by Ben Jones

Saving the Woods 67
by Bobbie Kinkead

When Rocks Offer Comfort 70
by Ethel Mays

Irish Twins 71
by Kelly Pollard

Mary and the Divine One 78
by Jennifer Lock

Lunch With Kitty 80
by Susan Mayall

blog spot...82
by sandra kay

Monoblogue..94
by David Collins

Adam 98
by Harold Gower

Andy 99
by Frank Thornburgh

Frank Rothman...105
by Harold Gower

Purple Orchids..106
by Diana Carey

Why I Write, Part II...110
by Selene Steese

The Journal...112
by Kathy Mima

The Picture 117
by Steve Workman

Robert Bly Changed My Life 126
by Pat Coyle

(familiarity)...130
by Ian Ray Armknecht

My Rightful Father 131
by Grace Ryan

Fatherhood...132
by Tom Darter

My Daughter's Wedding...134
by Charan Sue Wollard

Amber Afternoons 135
by Tania Selden

Sunday..136
by Jennifer Lock

My Parents' Bedroom 138
by Tania Selden

A Peach Cobbler Tale 139
by Karen L. Hogan

Government Cheerios 144
by Jennifer Lock

Before Smog 146
by Kathy Mima

Thunderheads 147
by Ethel Mays

Another Rain Poem 151
by Grace Ryan

Hangnails, ... 152
by Diana Carey

Empties 153
by J.D. Blair

caught up (9 of 12) 162
by sandra kay

Speed of Life 163
by Kathy Mima

Last Revolutionary War Widow Dies 164
by David Hardiman

The Chair *(excerpted from a longer story)* 167
by Selene Steese

Creature from the Black Lagoon 172
by Charan Sue Wollard

Saturday Evening in Harvard Square 173
by Grace Ryan

Voice Voyage 174
by Tom Darter

The Unannounced Visitor 176
by Karen L. Hogan

Why I Write, Part III 177
by Selene Steese

Anthology Contributors 181

Index of Authors 184

Foreword

by Rachael Lavezzo-Snedecor

What an honor to be asked to prepare this foreword for such an amazing literary celebration. As our Valley labors through the harvest of our grapes, olives, lavender, strawberries, pumpkins, ollalieberries, and so many other earthly treasures, it is with pride that I read each year the careful harvest of our local words. These written jewels are rich with the characteristics of the minds that formed them.

With hints of humor and shadows of tragedy, this book will take you on the journeys traveled by many feet.

Some will make you cry.

Some will make you laugh.

Some you will turn away from.

And some you will embrace.

But with each turn of the page, you will learn something new about your neighbors and fellow human beings. And, I dare say, I think you may even learn something about yourself.

These pieces are carefully selected each year by 4th Street Studio—a place where something happens, so something else can happen. If you are wondering what that means, then attend a Saturday Salon at 4th Street Studio, where people who write come and read aloud their thoughts and imaginative creations. The written word is always felt more deeply when read aloud by those whose thoughts and feelings were poured onto the page.

A few years back, while in England, I visited Shakespeare's Globe theater. On the wall was the quote:

"Let the Clapper, your tongue, be tossed so high, that all the house may ring of it!"

Enjoy these written words and, if you feel so moved, read them aloud. And may the whole of Livermore Valley ring with it!!

Rachael Lavezzo-Snedecor
Executive Director
Livermore Downtown, Inc.

A Story is Meant to be Passed Around

by Karen L. Hogan

My father's name was Bernard Hogan. His friends called him Hoagie or Ben. My cousins called him Uncle Bun; I never knew where that nickname came from.

He was a master electrician. He played golf. He was a storyteller. I don't think he knew he was a storyteller—he just had that gift for drawing you into his life experience. My bedtime stories were tales about his life on the farm in Cedar Rapids, Iowa. Stories about Buster, his collie, who liked to nip at the heels of the foul-tempered Shetland pony. Stories about swimming in the pond during the summer and skating on it in the winter. Stories about his father playing the fiddle at the Irish weddings and wakes, and on Sundays for the family while my grandmother accompanied him on the piano.

My grandmother would wake early and count the sleeping bodies nestled under mounds of bed covers before starting breakfast. There were ten children, but she never knew who had invited a friend to spend the night. The smells of bacon frying on the stove and biscuits baking in the oven were my father's alarm clock. He descended into that cloud of smells from the back staircase—the one that took him from the room he shared to the big rambling kitchen.

These tales of the olden days were my only link to my father's life before I was in it. My grandmother and grandfather had died long before I was born. My father, who was the seventh son and number nine in the line-up of ten, left the Midwest when he was seventeen to join the Navy.

My father openly, and I secretly, yearned for the life he had left behind. When we moved to Chico, California in the early sixties so my father could work on the Oroville Dam, we looked at a two-story house that had a back staircase leading to the kitchen. While my mother and father wandered through the rooms I stood on the porch and gazed out at the field, where I could just see a collie nipping at the heels of a foul-tempered Shetland pony. But my younger brother would have had to attend a one-room country school if we lived there, so my father's dream of regaining his past gave way to my parents' commitment to their children's future.

Of course there was also the other side to my father; the worldly, way-off-the-farm side. He would sit with me as I turned the pages of his leather-bound Navy album and tell me stories as I pointed to a picture.

The picture of a man wearing a grass skirt and a sailor's hat led to stories about crossing the equator. The picture of a bridge with a gap between two ends led to stories about San Francisco in the Thirties and of sailing into San Francisco Bay when the Golden Gate Bridge was still being constructed.

When I was three, Dad had a hard time finding work. He came home one day and asked my mother, "What would you think of living in Saudi Arabia?" Both of them were adventurous sorts, so my dad signed a contract with Aramco (Arabian American Oil Company) to work in Dhaharan, Saudi Arabia. He had to be there alone for two years so he could earn enough points to get family housing. His letters home told of foul-tempered camels, deserts called "The Empty Quarter," and Persian carpets spread out under tents setup in the desert for royal visits.

After we joined him he would sometimes leave for two or three days to work on "Explorations"—trips that took him deep into the desert. He would come back with stories about seeing a man eat locust, a Bedouin crossing the desert with his four wives—each on her own camel—and sand dunes the size of small mountains.

While we were in Arabia we alternated taking short vacations, which lasted two weeks, with long vacations, which lasted three months. For our long vacation my dad signed us up to travel to California on a Dutch freighter that carried only eight passengers. For 75 days we stopped at ports such as Bombay, Karachi, and Singapore as we made our way to Long Beach, California. Between the Philippines and Hawaii we sailed through the tail end of a typhoon with waves crashing over the top of the ship, which was as tall as a three-story building.

It was on that trip that my father first shared with me his love of sunsets at sea. He and I were the only passengers who never got seasick. So at times it was just him and me on deck, savoring the display of colors, which was different each evening; the sound of the ship, rising and falling, as it cut through the ocean; and the salty taste the sea sprayed on our lips.

And my father loved to play golf. He learned the game by caddying when he was a teenager. It was how he earned money when his family left the farm. An article in the *Sun and Flare*, Aramco's newsletter, titled "Arabia's own Ben Hogan," described the red golf balls he used so he could locate them on the barren, rocky course. I was six, and shortly after the article was published I saw a newsreel that included a story about Ben Hogan—the famous golfer. I looked at the newsreel, then at my dad, then back at the newsreel. I didn't understand why my dad looked so different up there on the big screen.

Through childhood and into high school I was my daddy's little girl. When I modeled the dress I was planning to wear to my first seventh-grade dance he told me I was "just like a breath of spring"—an image I resolved I would try to live up to. More than once he dreamily told me how much he looked forward to walking me down the aisle to hand me over to the man I would marry.

Then college happened. I started at San Francisco State in the fall of 1967, when the Vietnam War and the protests against it were rapidly escalating. During the second semester of my freshman year, Lyndon Johnson announced peace talks had begun and told us he would not seek a second term as president. It all seemed so hopeful. We had stopped the War, and Bobby Kennedy or Gene McCarthy would be our next president.

Then within a week, Martin Luther King was assassinated. Two months after that, so was Robert Kennedy. Three months later the Democrats held their convention in Chicago and nominated Hubert Humphrey, Johnson's hand-picked successor, instead of Gene McCarthy for the presidency. Protesters and police rioted.

By the Fall of 1968, Nixon was elected president, and my college went on strike. The charging police, rock-throwing protestors, and bloodied faces I had seen on television during the Chicago convention were now on my campus, in my face, accompanied by the sounds of breaking glass and billy clubs smashing against skulls, and the smells of tear gas and mace.

And of course there was the Women's Movement.

The world as I knew it was crumbling around me, changing too fast. I was angry. It was so different—and so uncharted—from the one I had been led to believe was real and secure. I saw no way that I could survive in this new world and continue to be the "breath of spring" my father wanted me to be.

When I was twenty-one, I married the man I had been living with for two years. I wore a décolleté wedding gown. A girlfriend who was a Universal Life Church minister performed the ceremony. I refused to let my father give me away, insisting that I was no one's to give away and no one's to be given to.

My father got the message. I was no longer his breath of spring. It wounded him deeply.

I began to see the dark cloud that hung over him, and I thought it meant that he was disappointed with me. So I became angry with him. My father's disappointment and my anger hung in the air between us for over a decade—a decade with no stories.

Signs of Alzheimer's began appearing in him when I was in my early thirties—about the time I was able to forgive him for being disappointed with me. During his moments of lucidity he started telling me stories again. But these were the other stories:

The men who got my grandfather drunk and cheated him out of the farm. My father, hearing my grandmother crying softly, watched the kitchen door grow smaller and smaller as he rode down the dirt road, passing for the last time the pond and the green field where Buster had nipped at the heels of the foul-tempered Shetland pony.

Adjustment to town life was brutal. Adults whispered and children taunted my father about my grandfather's foolish loss of the farm. There was no pond to swim in, no fields to roam through. Buster was my dad's only comfort. Then one day, when he was at school, my grandfather gave away Buster, telling my father, "Times are too tough for you to have a dog!"

That's when the beatings started. In a small, shame-filled voice my dad told me that he wet himself when my grandfather beat him and that the welts the strap raised on my father's back would take a week to heal.

The Navy had been my father's escape from my grandfather's brutality—and from what he had lost when he moved away from the farm.

The Depression was in full force when he got out of the Navy. He went two days without food. Just about the time he found work and was ready to start his life, Pearl Harbor was bombed. He rejoined the Navy to avoid being drafted into the infantry, and went to war. He never told me any war stories.

As the Alzheimer's slowly leeched my dad's spirit from his body, I resolved once more to be his breath of spring. I wanted to restore him to innocence. I wanted to reach what was left of him and replace the blasphemy of his father's brutality with the truth of love and gentleness. I did not want my father to leave this world until he was redeemed.

Instead, Alzheimer's spent the next ten years beating my father down. He turned into a terrified, confused child in an old man's body, and there were no more stories. My heart grew heavier with each visit, so my visits became more infrequent and shorter.

The day my mother called to tell me that he had forgotten how to swallow, I went to the nursing home knowing it was my last chance to bring him redemption. The nurse said he was being bathed. I found myself turning away from his room. With each step I took toward the door it became more clear to me: I had said everything and done everything I could for my father, but I had not saved him.

Once again I gave up trying to be his breath of spring. I settled for being by his side when he died.

On the day we planned to scatter his ashes, a friend called to tell me that she had had a dream about my father the previous night. They were on a boat on a body of water. As they looked out over the horizon at the setting sun, he told her how proud he was of me, that he admired my being a writer.

I was planning a trip to Ireland and decided I would take some of my dad's ashes with me, find a farm, and scatter them. I scooped some into a film canister; the rest we scattered on San Francisco Bay as the autumn sun was setting.

Three months later I was in Ireland. In pubs and in people's homes I heard stories (some true, some mostly true) about Celtic warriors, hedge schools, the Great Hunger, fiddlers and bards, and relatives in America. "I have a cousin in Chicago. Wouldcha know Kevin McCarthy, now?"

Each county seemed to have its own style of Irish craftsmanship: crystal, pewter, knits, and fiddleplaying.

In a pub in County Donegal, the northernmost county in the Republic of Ireland, I happened upon a festival of Donegal-style fiddling. Most of the older fiddlers could not read a note of music; the skill had been passed down to them from their fathers who had learned it from their grandfathers. I overheard a story of three sons playing their fiddles at their father's bed, conducting him to heaven, as he lay dying.

"Lovely! Lovely!" a gray-haired man exclaimed as a young man finished his tune, then handed him the fiddle. "A fiddle is meant to be passed around," he said and began playing.

I thought of my grandfather. He must have made music like this. What had twisted him so that hands that could express his soul through music instead betrayed my father with their brutality?

Memories of my father began flooding through me. Memories of the man I knew before the Alzheimer's turned him into someone else.

I remembered the kitten peeking out from his unbuttoned shirt as he emerged from the plane that returned him from an Exploration in the Empty Quarter. I have no idea how he found a kitten in a desert called the Empty Quarter.

I remembered the lights on the Highway Patrol car that pulled my dad over on our way back from Oroville. My Girl Scout troop had gone to visit the newly built dam—the one my father worked on. One of the girls from another car had lingered in the bathroom and been left behind. Without a complaint my dad turned around our 1960 turquoise Ford station wagon and drove the twenty miles back to Oroville to bring her home. He was the only father who was a member of my Girl Scout troop.

I remembered that he would make pizzas, from dough to sauce, for my slumber parties and cast parties. He never said no when I asked if we could have the party at our house, and my teenage friends always found our home was a safe haven.

I remembered that when I was twenty-eight, divorced and trying to learn how to put up shelves in my apartment, he had given me an electric drill and sander on my birthday.

In that pub, surrounded by the sounds of the fiddle players, my heart understood. My father had never really been disappointed with me—he had only been disappointed that I could not be his breath of spring. And then he honored my independence by giving me power tools.

I forgave him ever wanting me to be his breath of spring. And I forgave myself for wanting from him something he never could find—that place in himself that believed he was loved.

Early morning light appeared through the windows, and the fiddlers fiddled on.

I woke the next day with one more vivid memory of my father—the special holder he made for the six-pack of beer he carried in his golf bag; it kept the beer cold through eighteen holes of golf.

That afternoon I drove to Malin Head, the northernmost tip of County Donegal, where I had been told I would find a golf course—one that overlooked the ocean. It was January and it was cold and windy, so I had the course to myself. I went to the fourteenth hole, where for the last time I watched the sun set at sea with my father, then I opened the film canister, poured the last of his ashes into my hand, and let the wind carry him out to sea.

Why I Write, Part I
by Selene Steese

I write to feel the pen pressed
between my fingers, to hear
the sound it makes as I push
its point across the paper. I write

for the smell of paper,
the smoothness of it, the sheen,
the vast expanse of possibility
beneath my hand. I write

to say to the world "I am,"
to buzz in the ears of anyone
paying attention, to track ink
from my gadfly feet
across the pristine sheet
of another's expectations. I write

to burst into blossom,
like a cherry tree
after a spring rain, to shower
down words like pink petals
on the slick, silver sidewalks
of imagination. I write

to rise in my own estimation,
to pole my way through swamps
of ink in paper boats
using my pen to push off
from the rocks, to get me unstuck
from the parenthetical mud. I write

because words are embossed on my bones
and must spill out and out and out, eternally.

I write because I must, because long ago
all choice in the matter was taken
from me. I write because it is the simplest
thing in the world, and the most complex. I write
to skate around the edges of possibility,
to differentiate myself from the crowd,
to become the egg in the carton
that the magician cracks open, the one
that the bird bursts out of and flies
over the heads of the audience, singing.

I write to celebrate the absolute brilliance
of being alive, to savor
this moment
and this
and this.

The Best Sports Play I Ever Saw Involved a Trombone

by David Collins

It must have been 1968 or '69, and Baylor was on the road to play Texas A&M at the Holler House, the vertical Thunderdome of a hell hole they call a basketball arena at A&M. I'm not a Baylor fan, but I was there with some people who were. The game was progressing about as noisily as a college basketball game should when a call or an elbow or something sets somebody off, and one player punches another and the fight is on. All ten guys throw themselves at it like they always do. Whether they're fighting or trying to break it up never matters, and the benches empty onto the court.

The refs might have gotten control except some dimwitted fan feels compelled to take it public and leaps in and swings at somebody, which brings two hundred keyed-up spectators streaming onto the floor behind him, and the next thing you know the freaking Aggie Corps—in those days A&M was an all-male school and everybody was ROTC. If you were an Aggie, you were Corps—and the entire Corps is out of the stands onto the floor and the night is out of control.

I lean back in my seat looking for an exit sign, hoping I can get away before my friends drag me out there. Several hundred people are on the hardwood slugging it out and there's no stopping it, and lots of people are going to get suspended, and hurt and arrested, and Southwestern Conference Basketball is steering straight for the ditch.

It goes on for what seemed like minutes, though it was probably less than thirty seconds, when the smartest guy in the room stands up in the middle of the Aggie Band there in the bleachers. The band's as stunned as everybody else who's not on the court, except for this lone trombone player. He simply raises his instrument and starts to play. Nobody but the people sitting next to him can hear him, but they pick it up, and the people next to them catch on and join in and slowly the entire band comes to its feet and like John Phillip Sousa's soul rising from the grave, the national anthem warbles from that single horn into a full-throated roar above the riot.

As a unit, the Corps snaps to attention like a rubber band, a sudden bristling on the back of this huddled mass slugging it out on the floor and no more than two or three beats later it dawns on the rest of them that the fight's over, and in fifteen seconds 8000 people are standing rigid, and the only sound in the place is the last few bars of the Star Spangled Banner echoing off the walls. When the music dies away, everybody simply sits down and we're done, like it never happened.

Best damn sports play I ever saw.

Too Long Between Nothing and Something
by Timothy B. Rien

Eddie had walked a good two miles with his thumb out before he caught a ride from a cannery worker on rural 108. It was hot and the mosquitoes were up. Eddie was glad to be out of the sticky night even if the only relief was the balmy wind rushing through the car's broken window across his arm and face. He was headed to Jo Bell's card room.

The driver wouldn't shut up. Eddie wondered if the only conversation the guy could find was in the captive audience of hitchhikers. He had to hear about pasting labels on cans at Hunts, the two kids—one with a deformed thumb—and how much he owed the IRS. Eddie looked out the window. He had heard enough for one night. He had nothing to say. Mary had given him an ultimatum just before he left home that he needed time to work over in his mind.

He had been adjusting the contrast and color and brightness on his new, stolen television when Mary said that she wanted the damn thing out before she got home. She was dressed in loose panties and a bra and glared at him while she ironed her best white shirt—thread-bare, long sleeved cotton with a couple of cracked buttons and yellow stained cuffs. She was late to work so she was moving like the flickering light over an old movie screen. Her hands shook. Red ash crept up the cigarette in her mouth and every so often she pushed ringlets of dirty blonde hair from her eyes with the back of her hand. They tumbled back and she brushed them off again.

When Eddie had the picture just about right, he told her that it was their new entertainment center.

"It's another one of your cop magnets," she yelled. "I'm tired, Eddie. I'm tired of them busting doors and trashing our home."

She worked graves in the basement laundry at St. Elizabeth's Dominican Hospital where she loaded piss-stained sheets and blood-soaked pillowcases and towels into fifty-gallon washing machines. Once a week, she snuck their laundry in but by the time she had it smuggled back home, the shirts and sheets were wrinkled and looking pretty much the way she had taken them in. By the time she got home at dawn, she was in no mood.

"It's just a loaner," Eddie told her.

"Everything's on loan," Mary said. "I want it out." She set the iron upright. It hissed. "You get thrown in the can one more time and I'm leaving your lying, thieving ass."

He tried to tell her not to worry but he knew better—he was a worry. Though he didn't think of himself as a thief—or a liar. Those were her words, always the same two in the same breath, rushing in moments of towering anxiety or when she was tweaking. He thought of himself, instead, as someone sensitive to another person's feelings, a charitable guy. As far as Eddie was concerned, saying just the right thing was a matter of merciful kindness.

He had a job for a while at Do It Over Recycling just off River Road where he hoisted wire baskets loaded with aluminum cans on to a scale. Then he crushed them in a hydraulic press, filled-out little pink receipts and handed the customer cash. He liked chatting up world politics while the cans collapsed into little flat disks. What he knew of the world came from the *Oakdale Leader*, a local newspaper that carried nothing of world news other than irate letters to the editor. Eddie felt the appreciation of his customers for his lofty opinions.

But Eddie did not tell Mary that he had been canned. His boss found what she called "irreconcilable differences" between the little pink slips and the amount of cash paid out. He told Mary that his boss had insisted that he take a little time off because his lower back was beginning to feel the wear of his hard work. She raised her eyebrows at that, but Eddie wasn't going to be bothered about whether she believed him or not.

Besides, he found other gainful employment. He borrowed parts from tractors that he found parked in alfalfa fields or almond orchards. He'd strip them down and sell the parts to repair shops in a kind of life cycle that had the owners in the next day buying what had been lost the night before. Tonight wouldn't have been the time to tell Mary that.

It was approaching midnight when Eddie was dumped off at Jo Bell's card room. His neck itched. He buttoned the middle button of his shirt, pitched a flask into the bushes outside the front door and stepped in. It stank of stale beer and cigarettes. Eddie had a warm buzz on. He watched two men and a woman flipping cards into the center of a felt covered table. The woman was fingering chips like a tiny accordion.

Eddie leaned on the bar. There was a broken lottery machine there. He scratched at his neck and asked for a Jack straight up. Eddie hated the bartender, mostly for his pretense at liking him. He liked Jack Daniels. He liked it here and he liked it at home. Mary liked it too. She would stash a bottle of it in her underwear drawer every now and then. And every now and then he would find it, drink it and tell her later that she must have been high thinking she had hidden it there. He would never invade the privacy of her underwear drawer.

"Ante up before you start the shuffle there, mister man," said the baldheaded man. The guy next to him did not look up. He pushed in a couple of chips and shuffled the deck again. He scratched his belly. The woman smiled and met the bet. She was wearing a black lacy top that showed the fullness of her breasts. Eddie watched as the three of them played. The woman's chest swelled when she sighed to call or fold. He wondered what this woman might be like in some other place—maybe a grocery store. He could see the two of them pushing a shopping cart, arm in arm, through the frozen food section and talking about what they might share in a fine late-night dinner. He had never seen this woman before but he had the growing sense that she might be right for him. She looked over and smiled. Her teeth were yellowed and dull.

The other man at the table looked stupid. Eddie could read faces. He prided himself on this God-given instinct. The woman reached over and slid two blue chips to the center of the table for the stupid one. The man thanked her with a lolling nod and scratched at his belly. Eddie guessed that they must have come to the card room together because she was so attentive, but that he was nothing without her.

The bald man picked up a bottle of beer and blew into the top of it like a whistle. "Feel like killin' for money?" he said as if speaking into a microphone.

"I do," the woman said. Her voice was raspy.

She turned to the stupid one and, with the back of her hand, slapped him hard on the shoulder of his leather jacket. The smack stunned Eddie.

"You do, too," she said. The stupid guy lifted his head and let it fall.

In that brief moment the woman seemed to change. Eddie could now picture her barking orders while he pushed the shopping cart at a furious pace out in front of her. She would have him load the cart with beer and cigarettes and flour tortillas. He imagined that she would not speak to him until arriving at the checkout stand where she would grab an *Enquirer*, a pack of Camels and sunflower seeds, point to his wallet, and demand that he ante up.

Mary was not like that, he thought. She had no accounts to settle. Her life had always been plain and hard, but true. It was the true side of her that attracted Eddie most, and it was the true side that gave him the most to worry for.

Mary had been simple-drunk and happy that day she leaned on Eddie's arm in the pinkish light of the Tahoe wedding chapel. She coughed weakly and smiled up at him with her crooked little teeth, black and rotted at the edges. Eddie smiled back. They had elected the solemnity of a stand-up wedding, even though the chapel offered the convenience of a drive-through. In either case, the right Reverend Elvis would perform the ceremony.

They were half hung from the night before but Mary held steady, her eyes red-rimmed and glassy. The only guests had been Eddie's grandmother and her friend, Ralph—who was suffering a slow recovery from a knife wound to his leg. The high-collared Reverend Elvis gathered four or five employees from the funeral home next door to help fill the room. They were a cheerful bunch, chatting it up and teasing one another. Eddie estimated that these nice people were not so new to weddings.

Reverend Elvis asked everyone to stand. Eddie kissed Mary lightly on the temple. They promised each other a life until death, steadfast devotion through addiction and health, poverty and golden good luck. Eddie knew they were already living somewhere precariously between all of that.

As he turned to leave the chapel, Eddie noticed a tear that had gathered mascara just below Mary's eye. He smiled at her, took in the crisp, piney mountain air and led her down the wooden steps of the chapel. Pre-recorded chapel chimes rang, *ding-ding, ding-ding*. Everyone clapped and from nowhere came a shower of white rice. Eddie ducked and pretended he was running for a waiting limousine. Instead, they climbed into a rusted '68 Rambler with Brown Derby beer cans tied to the bumper by gimpy old Ralph. They laughed and the speakers on the chapel belted out, "Don't be cruel, to a heart that's true, I don't want no other love…"

As they drove off, Mary reached over Eddie and pumped on the horn and waved to Reverend Elvis. He waved along with all of the wedding guests, his white cape fluttering and glittering in the new day sun. They were so kind, all of them. Eddie loved the sound of that sputtering horn, the unpredictability of Mary, and the promises they had made that day. They smoked and sipped Jack with the windows down all the way to their reception at the nickel machines and poker tables at Harvey's in Reno. Eddie won over a hundred dollars, and felt that his life with Mary was off to a fine and prosperous start. Mary powder-packed her nose to keep that first day alive.

She was still racing the next morning when Eddie opened his eyes. She was sitting on the edge of the bed with the remnants of mascara smeared under one eye. She handed him a fragile black and white paper flower she had fashioned from the label of a Jack Daniel's bottle and told him how much she loved him.

"Hey there, sugar lips," the woman said.
Eddie smiled back at her.
"Get over here and spread some love."
Eddie pulled up a chair. He was feeling it. He could see himself flush with cash in about an hour. He leaned over and pulled a check from his back pocket, a little primer for the pump. "I'll need somebody to spot me some cash," he said.
"Sign it over," the bald man said.
Eddie wrote Mary's name across the back of the St. Elizabeth's check and collected four blue and three red chips.
Over the next hour, Eddie won and lost chips in silence. He began to feel the anxiety of living too long between nothing and something. Mary would be home soon. He needed to be there, and he needed to have something to show for the investment of her check. It had been stashed in the same underwear drawer as the Jack. Win or lose, he had some fat explaining to do.
On the next deal he decided to push all but one chip to the center of the table. And he did. "Another Jack," he called over his shoulder. "Straight up."
The woman smiled. Eddie could see she admired his bold character and decisiveness. That might be something she would like in a man, he thought. The stupid one next to her was a stooge—somebody that must have felt good for her to push around—but only satisfying to a point. He did not smile back. He flipped his cards.
"A full house," the bald man said. "You're all losers. Killing ya' for money. Pass me those chips." He laughed and looked up to the ceiling where wings of peeling paint fluttered above the fan.
Eddie felt a stabbing in his chest. He had one chip left. Mary would be home soon, and these people did not seem like the type to let money walk out the door. Eddie pushed back from the table and watched. He sipped at his drink until his speech was near-gone and his courage restored. Then he pulled his chair back in, looked at the woman and winked.
The bald man shuffled the cards. His forearms flexed. Eddie polished his last chip on his chest, kissed it and tossed it to the middle of the table. "Ante up *before* you shuffle, asshole,"

Eddie heard himself say.

The woman's eyebrows rose. Eddie felt heroic. She liked him. He knew it now.

Then Eddie noticed that the bald man had a black teardrop tattooed below his left eye. He wondered why someone would want to be reminded of their own sadness every time they looked into a mirror.

"I ought to cut you, mister man," the bald man said.

The woman took a long drag on a Lucky Strike cigarette. She waved it in the air, the smoke trailing like a festival banner. "Do it!" she said. "I'd pay to see that. Go ahead, cut him!"

The stupid one was suddenly awake. Wide, watery eyes. He scratched at his stubbled chin and then his belly. The bald man leaned back in his chair and withdrew a long, rusted Bowie knife from his boot. It had a faint glint along the cutting edge and at the tip. He laid it on the table in front of him with the delicacy of a surgeon.

Eddie was confused. This wasn't the woman he thought he knew. He pushed away from the table and stood. The knife rocked. The yellow flickering light from the fan made Eddie dizzy. His legs felt traitorous. He shuffled along the bar to the door. Stopped and stared into the emptiness outside and then briefly back. Everyone was smiling at him. Eddie was suddenly terrified. He did not want to go, and he did not want to stay.

Eddie hated playing games. As a boy he did not like taking turns, waiting in lines or sharing. He had always been past all that. But when he was twelve, his grandmother talked him into a year of little league baseball. It was something that came to him every once in a while as the worst and the best thing he had ever done. He would remember an early spring day when the sun shone bright but was intermittently hot and cold as billowing white clouds passed in front of it. Shadows swam like a great black fish over the bleachers, the dugout, the infield and pitcher's mound. It rolled out across the outfield and over the fence. Eddie could smell the wet clumps of freshly cut grass that littered the field. His uniform was filthy from the talcum-fine dust of the infield.

He had hit a homerun that day. He would never forget the clean, solid feel of a fastball leaping off the sweet spot of the bat. It had never happened before. Hoots and whistles filled the park as he rounded the bases. When he touched third, it finally occurred to him there was clapping, dozens of hands coming together from the stands—that sharp, scattered sound that a rushing river makes. His teammates were jumping in the dugout. It was a game-winning drive. A grand celebration. And it was all for him.

Eddie did not want to touch home plate and have it all end. He wanted to live the rest of his life right there—between third and home. But it wasn't to be. As he passed over the plate, and the clapping subsided, the catcher punched at the pocket of his glove with a closed fist, spit and, in a tight breath, said: "Once in a lifetime, Eddie. Suck my dick."

Eddie surveyed the stands for his grandmother that day, but she wasn't there. His teammates had already turned from the edge of the dugout and were walking back to the bench. He couldn't see any of their faces. And, at twelve, he had the first sense that real living was short.

The heat had not let up. Eddie stripped off his cotton shirt and tied it around his waist as he walked away from Jo Bell's card room. The parking lot at the Quik Stop was empty. There were lights on poles that cast a yellow pallor over everything. He could smell rotted vegetables and curdled milk from a dumpster on the side of the building. A raccoon raced away like a football player with something tucked under its arm.

Eddie walked through the front door. He heard a familiar *ding-ding, ding-ding.* His head was boozy and spun as he shuffled by the clerk, a slender Asian man perched behind the counter on a tall stool, his bare feet and thongs dangling helplessly.

Eddie thought for a moment about asking for a bottle of Jack from the wall behind the man. But the clerk wouldn't look out from behind a magazine that he had pulled close to his face. Eddie felt the clerk was having the same trouble seeing as he was.

He turned and looked back toward the door. He thought for a moment that the world had come to a blinding stop. There was a sputtering pink neon sign hung in the window facing out to the parking lot. It was an advert featuring a smiling bear hopping above a crackling fire. There was something written backwards beneath it but Eddie could not make it out. As the little bear hopped, Eddie struggled to remember why he was even there. He walked up the aisle toward an ice machine and sat on the floor in front of a shelf stocked with coffee. He had not felt this trashed in a long time and he thought he might need coffee. He pondered as if making a shopping decision, rubbed his hair and then picked up a jar of Taster's Choice and tried to read the label. The print was too small and looked smeared. He set it down on the floor and shivered as the air conditioning began to dry the perspiration on his bare arms and back and chest.

He looked around for his shirt. There were dust motes and sunflower seeds on the floor but he could not find his shirt. He last remembered having it as he crossed Second Street, passing the railroad station where he had stopped to relieve himself in an artful series of wet loops on the back of the station wall.

Then Eddie heard, *ding-ding . . . ding-ding.* Something about the bells reminded Eddie that he needed to get home, and he needed to get there now.

He gathered himself to his knees and started to stand when, from the other side of the store, Eddie heard a man say, "Whatcha ya readin' there, mister man?"

The clerk was talking so fast, Eddie could not make out what he was saying. It was something about children, a wife, a mother.

"Oh, just do it," Eddie heard a woman say. "Cut him."

Eddie had this recurrent nightmare. He never thought enough of it to tell Mary, but it always startled him awake. It was twilight. A muggy evening. He would be sitting in the hammock on his little broken porch watching bats flutter with blinding speed across the surface of the lazy river below. As the moon rose, the bats would disappear. Then he would hear Mary cough that little cough of hers. When he turned she would be leaning in the doorframe behind him picking a piece of tobacco off the tip of her tongue. She would take a long drag from a cigarette and say she was leaving, going to Albuquerque or Tucson or Phoenix with a truck driver named Javier. Never the same place, but always Javier. She would explain that she didn't love Eddie the way she used to.

When he thought about that dream, Eddie realized that he had grown accustomed to the fear of Mary disappearing—just like that. She had, of course, never said she was done loving him, but that nighttime fear was, nonetheless, paralyzing. By morning the feeling would pass and Eddie would go about another day.

Now, something was happening and Eddie couldn't see it. Two people were demanding money from the clerk and threatening him with a knife, and they were standing between him and the front door. Eddie didn't want to move. He began to shake. He shook so hard he could no longer sit still. He rolled to his knees and crawled to the ice machine. He curled there and shook against the cold metal box.

Eddie's mother died when he was five weeks old. He was never really told how she died, but he came to understand that it had something to do with him. When he was six, his grandmother took him to the railroad station to see his father off. "He'll be back," she promised. She knelt down and steadied him by the shoulders. "It's his mind," she said looking

Eddie in the eyes. What Eddie did not know at that moment was that his father was leaving for drug rehab and would never return. As the train pulled away, Eddie's father leaned from the window and waved at him. His father smiled and held the top of his hat against the unsettling force of the wind. The expression on his face was puzzling. It was as if this act of leaving had some mysterious element of joy folded into it, something Eddie was not privy to. He felt as if the train had been tied to a spool of yarn nestled in his chest. As it pulled away something got smaller and smaller until Eddie felt a stabbing pain between his ribs. He knew then he would never see his father again and that the element of joy was a cruel trick.

Eddie heard the bells again. Then, it was quiet. Deadly quiet. They must be gone. He could see the reflection of the little bear hopping above the fire. The window began to flicker with traces of red and blue light. Something was happening to the happy bear. Eddie stood. He heard a wailing in the far distance and made his way to the door. There was no one at the counter but it was slick and shimmering in the light with each hop of the bear, and the floor in front of the counter was puddled black. When he reached the parking lot Eddie could see the red and blue flickering lights coming from beyond the train station. He ran.

He felt like he was running for his life but he didn't know where to go. He only knew to run for it. All he had ever felt at times like this was *get away*, never look back. And that was what he did. His feet grew heavy with every step and his heart pounded. He ran until he heard a siren whoop in the street behind him. Then he dived headlong into a shallow stand of junipers at the edge of the sidewalk. The stiff, thorny branches tore at his bare chest and arms and face as he fell to the cavernous space below. He was breathing hard and his head filled with the pungent and bitter odor of juniper.

Soon, there were voices screaming, "Killer." Shards of light penetrated the cover like knives on fire. They scoured the fine, powdery dirt around him and, finally, over him. "Do not make us come in there to get you!" someone yelled.

Eddie did not move. He lay face down with his head resting on an outstretched arm. He closed his eyes and drew a deep bitter breath. The shouts began to fade and the pain in his arms and chest began to fade too. He could now see himself somewhere else, perhaps asleep with Mary seated at the edge of the bed waiting for him to awake, the faint sound of paper tearing. But he did not want to open his eyes and find her gone.

The Day the Ice Cream Disappeared

by Susan Mayall

One day in 1942 the ice cream disappeared. It had never been a large part of our diet. For one thing, we didn't have a refrigerator, which wasn't particularly unusual in those days. It was cool enough most of the time in England for food to survive on a pantry shelf—though not, of course, ice cream. Even in wartime milk was delivered daily, and we shopped every day for meat, fruit, vegetables, which came from small shops just down the street. And they acquired it from local farms and suppliers, so it was fresh when we bought it. Potatoes still had dirt clinging to them, eggs often had smears of chicken droppings. And we knew the cows that produced our milk—they grazed in the fields just behind our house.

Ice cream was not the first of the favorite foods that had disappeared from our diets. It was just one of the most importance to Howard, Richard, and me. I was nine, Howard seven, Richard five. Since 1939, when the war started, we'd learned to live without bananas and lemons, grapefruits, and pineapples. We'd grown accustomed to cakes without icing, margarine instead of butter on our toast or sandwiches, tiny portions of meat, and no second helpings. But ice cream was a special treat, and until that day in 1942 it was something we looked forward to.

The day it disappeared was like most other days that sunny wartime summer. In Devon, where we'd moved when the bombing in Portsmouth got too bad, we didn't have an ice cream cart coming 'round each afternoon. Our ice creams came from Cole's dairy in the village. That summer we went to the beach almost every day. The dairy was on our way. It stood on the left-hand corner past the church, just before the paved road gave out and turned into a rocky lane between high banks. Opposite it was the village smithy, a destination in its own right. In a small, thatched building the blacksmith hammered red-hot horse shoes into shape on his anvil, and slapped them onto the hoofs of huge, patient work horses. We loved to watch him working, clad in his collarless shirt and waistcoat, a boy in corduroys and cloth cap wielding the bellows to keep the fire blazing.

But if we were making for the beach we didn't go to the smithy. We just stopped at the dairy. It was a barren place, bare walls and a counter, selling milk and eggs, a few dusty packages of biscuits, and ice cream. The ice cream was all vanilla, and you ate it in a cornet (cone in American terminology) or a sandwich between two wafers. Or you could, as a special treat, have an ice cream soda. We had never had one 'til we went to Devon. In fact we never had fizzy drinks at all, so that in itself was exciting. A deep red cherry soda with a scoop of ice cream in it was true heaven, the best thing there was to eat at that time. Of course we didn't have one every time—they were more expensive than cones. We would sit at the rickety tables outside the dairy, with the singeing smell of the horses' hoofs in our nostrils, and slowly, rapturously spoon the sweet, creamy liquid into our mouths.

Recently, we had noticed that the ice cream had become less creamy, grayer in color. It didn't taste so good either, but the soda helped disguise the taste, and today we were going to have ice cream sodas. That was because, for the first time in a month or so, we'd been kept awake by sirens and the hated, unsynchronized sound of German aircraft engines. In the distance was the crump of bombs exploding, not enough to shake the house or send us to the cellar, but enough to remind me of the raids in Portsmouth. We had all ended up in my mother's bed, where she made animal shadows on the wall in the glow of her flashlight. It was better than being alone, but I still couldn't talk or move, intent as I was on listening to those dreaded sounds.

So when we got up, still a bit bleary eyed, my mother announced "Ice cream sodas today!"

We walked to the beach, of course. We'd never had a car, and in any case nobody did at that stage of the war, unless it was essential for some vital activity. Our baby sister Sarah was strapped into the big green pram we'd all used, then it was loaded with a picnic basket, beach balls and books, and finally towels and swim suits and a blanket—and sweaters to put on after our chilly swims. And we set off, out of our creaky green gate, down our street—the last before the fields began—and onto the road that led to the cliffs, the cove and the sea.

Howard, Richard, and I ran most of the way—we usually did—and this time we wanted to get to the dairy fast. My mother, pushing the heavy pram, came more slowly. Often, she ran too, on ordinary walks—she loved to race us. After my father's ship went down in 1941 she'd stopped running for awhile, and the way we knew she felt better was when, one day, she'd said, "Let's race!" So when, today, as we came into the village, she said, "Race you to the dairy!" we knew it would be a good day. She won, of course, and as we puffed up to the door she was already pushing it open.

"Morning, ducks!" said the lady behind the counter. "And what would you like today?"

"Three ice cream sodas and one small cornet, please, Mrs. Beets," my mother said.

"Sorry, love, no ice cream. Rules are rules—they say we can't make it no more. Uses too much cream, they say—bad for the war effort."

My mother looked down at us. I could tell she minded more than we did.

"It's all right, Mom—we can still have sodas," I said.

"It's sad for the kiddies," said Mrs. Beets. "Used to love ice cream myself when I was their age."

"Oh well!" said my mother. "Sodas all round! What color would you like, Howard?"

We had lime and orange and cherry. My mother even had one, too. We walked up the rocky lane to the open cliffs, hauled Sarah and the supplies down the cleft where the steps had been taken out to hinder German invaders. There was usually nobody else on the beach—people were still scared of hit and run raids. We spread the blanket on the sand, changed into our swim suits and dashed into the water. As usual the sandwiches, the cold new potatoes, the apples, or pears were crunchy with sand, but tasted better than any picnics ever since. We trudged home happily at the end of the day, our skins salty from the sea. "You won't need baths tonight after all that swimming," my mother said. The day became one like many others that summer and those that followed.

When ice cream reappeared soon after the war, we rode our bikes to the town to buy it from the first van to visit us. But I was twelve by then, and it never tasted as good as those ice cream sodas in the village.

What I remember most from those summers is the feel of sand between my toes, the joy of diving into the waves, the sun and wind on my face. And being hungry, truly hungry, so that everything tasted good, not just ice cream sodas but cold boiled potatoes and sandwiches thinly spread with margarine, and apples that often had worms in them.

My mother, the person who gave us those summers, was thirty-five years old at the time. She wasn't deterred by war or widowhood—she refused to let Hitler ruin her children's lives. Some things she couldn't change. But with a mother who raced us, who made animal shadows in the midst of air raids, who knew the value of ice cream sodas, how could we feel deprived?

Midnight in Texas
by Bryant Hoex

"Welcome to Texas, the Lone Star State." I read the sign aloud.

Rich's voice chimed in, "Yee-hah! We're in Texas, boy!"

"Well shee-howdy!" I retorted.

"Is this all there is?" Rich drawled, surveying the complete lack of scenery around us. "I thought everything was supposed to be big in Texas!"

"Big lot o' nothin'!"

"Hey boy . . . don't mess with Texas!" Rich said, and soon we raised a sarcastic chant, "The stars at night, are big and bright . . ."

Why the unprovoked animosity towards our fine southern friends, you ask? Good question. Wish I had a good answer. On the level of sports rivalries, there was plenty of cause to talk trash. As a 49er Faithful, Rich gleefully detested the Cowboys, while my beloved Sharks had equally intense bad blood with the Dallas Stars. Of course there was more . . . perhaps an assumption (well-thought out or not) that Texas, as a beacon of the South, stood for the opposite of what we had in California, that this was where we would find all those ignorant, backwoods, hick-town rednecks that married their own cousins and home-schooled their kids so they wouldn't be taught evolution. Never mind that the only four people I'd ever actually met from Texas lived in metropolitan areas and were fairly liberal and affluent . . . when one is determined to impose sweeping stereotypes, one cannot let facts stand in the way.

Barreling down the open road in our metallic baby-blue station-wagon (hardly the chick magnet we had envisioned cruising in; Hertz apparently had a twisted sense of humor), things had mellowed out after our initial flurry of obnoxiousness crossing the border. Our itinerary—enemy to all things spontaneous and wonderful about vacation, yet a necessary evil in this case—demanded that we make it halfway across Texas before stopping for the night, still leaving us a full-day's drive if we hoped to make it to New Orleans by Friday as planned.

Rich merged onto Interstate 20 and we continued east, with fewer and fewer drivers on the road as the hours wore on. It seemed as if the wide, divided highway had been built just for us—no taillights ahead of us or headlights coming up behind. The large grassy divide added to the enormous feel of the highway and the solitude that arose from being the only ones on it.

"Man, that center divide's as wide as a football field," noted Rich.

"Wanna get out and start a pick-up game?"

"Sure," he laughed. "Doesn't look like there's anyone around to join us, though."

He was right. It was just Rich and me and the open road, with a yawning expanse beckoning ahead of us.

Yet, something was amiss. I'd figured we would just be flying down the highway at this point, making up for lost time and possibly cutting some miles off tomorrow's drive to New Orleans . . . Rich, however, seemed to be in no particular hurry. I glanced at the speedometer, which stood at a steady 57. I thought of the long drive ahead of us the next day, but didn't want Rich to think I was criticizing his driving. Okay, internally I was criticizing his driving, but at the end of a long day I didn't think it wise to say anything negative. I sorted through my cassette case and popped another mix tape into the car stereo. I half-heartedly tried humming along, then sighed and turned on the cabin light, at which point I started tracing our route along the Texas map in my travel atlas. I looked again at the speedometer—57. Great. He had us on cruise control. I sighed once more and flicked off the light.

Rich had experienced this blatant subtlety of mine on more than one occasion. "Is something wrong?" he asked.

"No . . . well, it's just—do you think we could maybe go a little faster? We've got an awful long drive ahead of us tomorrow and this would be a great chance to make up some miles."

"Hey, I'm just making sure to stay around the speed limit. You saw the signs back there."

This was true. "Speed Limit 65 MPH", the top half had read, followed in equally-large font by "55 at Night." This made no sense. With no one else on the road, what was the danger? Were they afraid we might hit a raccoon, or maybe cripple an unsuspecting tumbleweed?

"I know, Rich, but come on . . . there's not a single car around in any direction. There's no one behind us for miles."

"Listen, when it's your turn to drive again, you can go as fast as you want. As for me, I have no desire to meet up with any Texas troopers tonight."

And that was that. Rich had spoken, and with a stubborn streak the size of . . . well, Texas

. . . he wasn't about to change his mind. (I did notice, however, that his finger had hit the "increase speed" button on the wheel one time, bringing us up to a whopping, warp-speed-esque 58 MPH.)

We crawled down the desolate highway for another hour or so until Rich, probably sensing that I was chomping at the bit, exhaled deliberately and said, "Man, I'm getting exhausted. You think you could take over in a little bit?"

"Yes!" came screaming from my mind down towards my mouth, but luckily it was tackled by my self-restraint and held down long enough for me to manage a short pause, followed by a nonchalant, "Yeah, sure, if you need me to,"

We switched positions outside a gas station mini-mart (the first we'd found in over a half-hour . . . you know you're in B.F.E. when you can't even find someone to sell you an overpriced soft drink) and shortly after eleven we were back on the highway. The atmosphere in the car seemed magically transformed. Of course, the energy surge we received from the caffeine and sugar we'd just inhaled probably wasn't hurting either. I was thrilled to be in the driver's seat, both figuratively and literally, and soon had us racing down the open road. Taking an occasional glance in the rear-view mirror, I was ready to ease off the accelerator at the first sign of headlights in the distance, but with none in sight it was all systems go. I popped in one of my favorite mixes, and we drowned ourselves in the Beastie Boys, Green Day, Chili Peppers, Sublime—songs full of attitude and testosterone—which blared out of the speakers. Released from the responsibility of focusing on the road, Rich seemed to loosen up as well, and soon we were shouting along at the top of our lungs, our own little moving party rolling across Texas.

I believe I have a musical memory . . . that is, I always remember what song was playing when a significant event occurred in my life. I can't tell you what time it was, what the weather was like, or what my high-school sweetheart and I were wearing when we shared our first kiss, but I sure as hell can tell you that "Just Like Heaven" by the Cure was playing on the radio. How appropriate, then, that after a mellow Sarah McLachlan tune had calmed Rich and I down a bit, it was the Cure's "Killing An Arab" that soon had us rocking in our seats again.

Our party was still in full motion; even Rich, who was always amused by my passion for alternative music but generally clueless when it came to the actual lyrics, was bouncing his head and shouting the parts he recognized. Robert Smith's edgy voice was railing . . . he could turn and walk away, he could fire the gun . . . when suddenly an instrument I hadn't noticed before chimed in. It was a siren.

At that exact same moment, the darkness of the wide center divide flashed to life in red and blue, and a Texas highway patrol car, which had been stealthily lying in wait, spun a quick U-turn and pulled onto the road behind us.

I looked anxiously over at Rich, with no other travelers within five miles of us in any direction, and asked in complete seriousness, "Are they coming after *us*?" That was probably one of the dumbest things that has ever come out of my mouth. The only reason I don't say it was the dumbest, in fact, is because that came a few minutes later.

Rich widened his eyes and stared back at me, his jaw hanging open. "Is there anyone else out here?" The flashing lights—accompanied now by high-beams—were upon us. The shock of the situation washed over me, my body kicked into auto-pilot and pulled the car over onto the shoulder.

As the police car rolled to a slow stop behind us, my internal self-flogging had already begun: Rich warned me, I thought I knew better, so now I was going to get a ticket. Served me right. At this point I became aware of the loud music still blaring, almost mocking me with the fun I'd been enjoying just a few moments ago. Wanting to turn it off but unable to think clearly, I simply shut off the engine. The party was definitely over.

I'd like to say I remember the look on the officer's face when he first got out of his patrol car, but I was so blinded by the bright searchlight trained on us that all I could make out was a tall shadow striding towards us. Soon I heard boots on gravel, and the largest police officer I'd ever seen was staring down at me through my window. Maybe it was true about everything being big in Texas.

"Good evening," he boomed. "How are you boys doing tonight?"

"Um, fine, sir, thank you." Where did sir come from?

"Do you know how fast you were driving?"

Truth be told, I didn't know, though it had to be at least in the seventies. "No sir, I don't." He paused, so I added, "Was I speeding?" Nice touch.

"I clocked you doing 82 miles an hour, and this is a 55 zone at night."

He had me. I was busted. This was a moment that might have made lesser men crumble, but I somehow found it within me. After only the slightest pause, I let my eyes grow wide and gave what Rich to this day calls the greatest acting performance of my entire career.

"Eighty-two? Oh my God . . . thank you. I'm so glad you pulled me over! (sigh) I had no idea. What . . . 82? That's so unsafe! I'm sorry . . . I knew we should have pulled over at the last town, but I just hoped we could make it a little further. You see, we've been driving all day and I'm just so tired that I didn't even realize how fast we'd gotten up to. It's really good that you stopped me."

Looking into my Bambi-eyes, the cop nodded his head. Nodding was good. Maybe he was sympathetic.

Or maybe he was just confirming in his mind that I was totally full of shit.

"I'm gonna need to see your license and registration."

"Well, this is a rental car, sir, but I'm guessing it's in the glove compartment. Can we look?" He nodded again, his hand hovering near his gun, while Rich slowly opened the glove compartment and handed over the vehicle's paperwork. I cautiously retrieved my wallet and handed him my driver's license.

A quizzical look crossed his face as he read it. "It says here you're from California?"

"Yes sir," I replied, "we're in the middle of a cross-country vacation."

He looked at me as if he'd never heard of such a concept. Then again, perhaps he was just confused by my sudden shift into telling the truth.

"You boys stay here for a minute; I need to take these documents back to my car and run them through our system."

Fair enough, I thought . . . that was standard procedure. I wondered how much this was going to cost me. Having lost more money in Vegas than planned, and with a night in New Orleans and five days at Disneyworld left to pay for, I could already imagine munching on granola bars in the station wagon instead of eating out for the next week.

I looked over at Rich, whose eyes had apparently rolled into the back of his head during my earlier sob story. "What do you think he's gonna do? You think we're gonna get a ticket?"

"I don't know," Rich shook his head grimly. "I'm not sure. Probably." Our concern grew as the officer stayed back at his car longer and longer.

"What is he doing back there?" I finally wondered aloud, turning around and trying to glimpse what was going on—impossible through the intense search lights. "He should already have come back by now." My hopes that I might escape without a ticket dwindled.

We waited in quiet desperation as the minutes dragged on, our only company the sound of crickets and an occasional incomprehensible voice blurting over the police radio transmitter. At last we heard the slam of a car door behind us, and the hulking officer soon appeared again at my window. Blonde hair, pale skin, muscles nearly bursting through his police uniform, and large hands that were . . . wait. Empty? Where was my ticket? Come to think of it, where was my license? I looked at the officer with what was now genuine confusion, and he responded by bending down towards us and announcing, "I'm gonna need you boys to step out of the ve-hicle." He looked past me to Rich. "You too."

Rich and I exchanged horrified glances. What was going on? My fear and confusion were matched only by my sense of guilt; up until now had I thought it would be just me who was going to pay for my mistake, but now Rich was being pulled into this mess as well.

We got out of the car nervously—I noticed Rich didn't have any "shee-howdy"s or southern drawls to share with the officer either—and suddenly what had been only an act earlier was becoming very real: we were frightened tourists, out of our league and in real possible danger. We were far from home, out in the middle of nowhere with no one to defend us, and these cops suspected us of something. My first hope was that this might just be a sobriety test, which I would pass with flying colors unless I was too terrified to walk in a straight line. I noticed, however, that the trooper's younger partner had greeted Rich on the other side of the car and started to ask him some questions.

This left me alone with the Herculean officer, and he wasted no time in striking up a conversation. "So you say you're on vacation?" I nodded. "Where'd you boys start your trip?"

Figuring he hadn't heard of Mountain View, I answered "San Francisco . . . the Bay Area."

"And where are you boys planning to drive to tomorrow?"

"New Orleans."

"Where were you earlier today?"

"Carlsbad Caverns."

"Where are you planning to end up?"

"Florida"

"And what are y'all going to be doing there?"

"Spending five days at Disneyworld." What was I, a travel agent? If he was looking for some hot vacation tips, he surely could have found a more qualified person to ask.

When he had finished grilling me with a few more questions about our itinerary, he gestured to his partner and they switched places. His partner looked like the prototype rookie: younger, leaner, less deliberate, and with an air of nervous excitement, as if he couldn't believe he was finally getting to bust some tourists.

As he proceeded to drill me with the same questions his veteran partner had just asked, it all started to come together in my mind. We had California driver's licenses, a rental car with New Hampshire license plates, and we had just been stopped going over 80 MPH in Texas around midnight. Of course it looked like we were up to something. As I robotically answered the officer's questions, my eyes fixed on all the suitcases and bags in the back of the station wagon. Did they actually think . . . ?

"All right, boys," my train of thought was interrupted by Officer Mammoth, who had finished with Rich and brought him around the car to stand next to me. "I'm going to ask you a question and I'm only going to ask this one time: Do either of you have any illegal substances in this here ve-hicle?"

It was time for everyone's favorite game show: How Well Do You Know Your Friends? Luckily Rich and I were like brothers. "No officer," I fairly blurted out, "neither one of us does drugs. I'm a teacher and I know how much trouble I could get in for doing that stuff."

Now, for most people that would have been enough of an answer, but my brain happens to be of an incredibly unique constitution. While in most regards a well-oiled machine, noble in reason and infinite in scope, if the size of my brain were proportional to the amount of common sense I possess, it would sit comfortably on the head of a pin. This seems to be the only plausible explanation for the sentence that followed.

"You can search the car if you want."

My confident voice trailed down as I realized too late how this might totally backfire. What was I thinking? The officer stepped back and looked at me, apparently as amazed by my stupidity as I was, then excused himself and retreated slowly to the patrol car.

Had my explanation actually worked? I wondered as we stood there in the high beams. Perhaps through some pathetic sense of pity or sheer shock value, he had decided to back off and end the inquisition? That's it, I thought. Always confuse the enemy.

Our momentary peace was short-lived. Bigfoot promptly returned with a clipboard in his hand. "Could you please sign this?" he asked with a tone that let me know he could ask less politely if I happened to refuse.

"What is it?" As if I needed to be told.

"It's a warrant giving us permission to search your ve-hicle." He couldn't resist rubbing it in, adding, "Since you said it would be OK."

"Oh? Oh! Of course!" I replied with all the self-assurance I could exude, locking my tunnel-vision on the signature line and trying to remember how to spell my name.

"I'm also going to need your keys."

This was a request I'd never heard before, but I obliged and hoped he wouldn't notice the shaking hand that offered them. I then took a step back and prepared to watch the two Texas Titans search the car and confirm our innocence. Unfortunately we weren't going to be afforded such a close-up view.

"I'll need you boys to follow me."

I shot a quick glance over at Rich, whose puzzled look back seemed to indicate your guess is as good as mine. There were also probably several other thoughts going through his mind about me as well, though I chose not to consider what those might be.

The officer guided us over towards the edge of the shoulder, where the pavement abruptly ended and dropped off into a shallow valley of dirt below. He then spoke the words that will forever be etched in my memory.

"Can you boys please step down into the ditch?"

As I looked over the edge, my breath caught—not at the physical depth, which was a mere four feet and an easy jump down—but rather at the helplessness of our situation. Saying no was not an option, but I was acutely aware that history has not been kind to those who have been asked to step down into ditches, particularly when followed closely by armed men.

"Is it OK if we just stand over here and wait by the edge?" I hoped he might allow this small compromise. After all, he had our keys. Where were we going to go?

"I'm sorry, but I'm going to need you to step all the way down." I looked over at Rich, already solemnly lowering himself in, and realized there was no avoiding it. Our fate was sealed. I descended with all the dignity a terrified California boy could muster and turned to face our oppressor. Standing chest-high in the dusty chasm, I felt even more Lilliputian gazing up at his imposing six-and-a-half foot frame, his broad shoulders and chiseled jaw outlined by the black Texas midnight. What would happen now? His hand was on his hip—right next to his pistol—and it would only take one pull of his trigger to bring all the hopes and dreams of my twenty-eight years to an abrupt end in a Texas ditch, with no one around to see or hear.

What possible reason would he have to hurt us, though, my logic questioned.

My anxiety (always better at winning arguments like these) immediately fired off a plethora of reasons: malice, corruption, hatred of all things Californian, some backwoods-hick ritual of proving one's manhood by killing innocent tourists . . . even worse, I'd told him we were from San Francisco. Two men traveling together . . . oh God, what stereotypes did he have of us? I wondered how long it would take for anyone to find our bodies. Would anyone truly make a genuine effort to track down our assailants?

"You boys just stay here while we search the ve-hicle." I was jolted back to the present just in time to see the officer join his partner as they turned their attention to our rental car-toon. The thought of that ridiculous baby-blue station-wagon sedan being used by drug smugglers was laughable, though the humor was a bit difficult to appreciate at the moment.

With the officers busily attending to our ve-hicle, I was able for the first time to reflect on our situation. My first fear—of being violently executed terrorist-style—was quickly abating, and I took what was the closest to a normal breath I'd had in ten minutes. Visions of circling vultures and crime scene investigators, arriving a week later when clued in by the smell of rotting flesh, began to dissipate, but were soon replaced by a new and more plausible—hence more frightening—thought: what if these cops really were in some way corrupt and decided to plant something in the back of the station wagon?

I turned to Rich, who not surprisingly was masking his fear much better than I had been. He was steeled in a quiet intensity, and while I feared his rightful wrath for having dragged him down (literally) into this situation, I needed to escape from the horrific visions in my imagination and talk to him . . . maybe I could ground myself in reality again.

"Do you think this is legit?" I whispered.

He turned towards me, keeping his gaze averted. "Too late to matter now, isn't it?"

So much for comfort. To his credit, Rich knew the power of his angry stare—a cold, steel gaze that could look through your eyes, bounce off the back of your skull, and suck all your self-confidence with it on the way back out—so, like a thoughtful hunter with a loaded weapon, he had made sure not to point it directly at me.

Merciful though this gesture was, it left me alone again, trapped in my head and at the mercy of my swirling thoughts. How had I allowed this to happen? The soundtrack in my mind became a lost verse from the Talking Heads, with David Byrne ranting, "And you might find yourself standing in a Texas ditch. On a beautiful night. And you might ask yourself, well . . . how did I get here?"

How did I get here indeed. Just minutes ago I had been the lord of my own universe, master of my domain, free as a twenty-something single man could be, on vacation and traveling wherever my heart desired. Then, through sheer . . . what was it? Impatience? Pride? Desire to prove a point to a friend? Subconscious need to create outer drama to match my inner turmoil?

Damn that therapist . . . I now found myself—and my entire future, potentially—at the mercy of a Texas trooper who had no reason to do me any favors. My continued independence and career depended on the integrity of a man whom I didn't know from Adam, other than to say he was much more intimidating and packing heat. The loss of autonomy is an incredibly frightening proposition in any case—a terrifying helplessness many face as they age—but even worse when caused by one's own choices. Like the person in the doctor's office waiting for their HIV results thinks back ruefully to the moment before he or she indulged in that ill-advised one-night stand, like the unhappily married mother of three thinks back to her wedding morning, when she ignored her gut feeling and said "I do," I finally appreciated the freedom I'd enjoyed behind the wheel now that I'd been relegated to the passenger seat.

Meanwhile, the rookie cop was zealously opening and inspecting every bag, jacket pocket, and piece of luggage he could get his hands on. His efforts were rewarded with nothing but unwashed drawers and socks mixed with scattered souvenirs, but this didn't seem to dampen his enthusiasm for his work. (Come to think of it, I suppose I'm lucky he didn't pull the film out of my camera in case I'd somehow inadvertently taken a picture of some narcotics back in New Mexico.) His veteran partner, by contrast, wore an expression that seemed to indicate partial boredom and—could it be?—mild amusement, half-heartedly flipping a jacket over with his nightstick while he waited for his partner to finish his search. This certainly wasn't how I remembered seeing it on *Cops*, but by this time I began to sense that they didn't exactly view us as much of a threat. It probably helped that we were (a) white, (b) innocent, and (c) so incapable of holding poker faces that if we had been guilty we would have already pissed our pants and shown them the drugs ourselves. In any case, this search wasn't exactly something I would have chosen to watch in prime time, but, standing there in the ditch, it was the only channel on.

Soon a husky pair of legs came striding over towards our bunker of shame and stopped inches away from my ghostly-white face. "You boys can come on out now."

I looked up to see a strong arm extended in my direction. I grabbed hold of it to pull myself up, then soon realized that I was being pulled and unless I wanted my arm separated from its socket, I'd better bring the rest of my body along as quickly as possible.

Grateful to be back on ground level, my relief overpowered a vague feeling that I still hadn't regained my original height. Standing face-to-chest with the officer, I tilted my head upward and saw that he had yet another surprise for us . . . a smile.

"I wanna thank you boys for your cooperation in this matter, and I'm gonna do you a big favor: I'm gonna let you boys off with just a warning tonight."

Oh my God, of course . . . he could have easily given me a ticket! That original dread which struck me when I first saw the flashing lights had already been forgotten, trivialized by the greater fears which had taken its place down in that ditch.

"The next town up here is Abilene," the officer continued. "I'd suggest you boys pull off there and find yourselves a place to spend the night. Just so you know, there's another Highway Patrol station right beyond Abilene, and I don't think y'all want to be meeting any more of us tonight."

"Oh no . . . I mean, yes, yes, we definitely will stop in Abilene. We were planning on stopping at the next city anyway. Yes, that works great," My head bounced rapidly up and down like an overly springy bobblehead doll.

With a wide grin, the trooper offered his enormous hand to me; shaking it, my palm momentarily disappeared inside his, as if caught inside a baseball glove. He repeated the gesture with Rich, then nodded towards us one last time. "You boys have a good night."

We overenthusiastically reciprocated his well-wishes, and he turned and headed back to his patrol car. I staggered numbly over towards the driver's side of our rental beast, feeling something was missing. What was it? Oh yes, now I realized . . . my testicles! A cocky, naïve out-of-towner from the West Coast had stopped here twenty minutes earlier; now a wide-eyed, shaken, emasculated twin took his place behind the wheel.

I realized that Rich and I weren't exactly alone yet; the officer was parked behind us and waiting patiently for me to get out on the road again, after which I presumed he'd follow us just long enough to ensure I would drive below the speed limit, with my hands at ten and two, until he decided I'd had enough humiliation for one evening.

I fastened my seat belt and took a deep breath. I calmly adjusted the mirror to get the glaring headlights out of my eyes. I coolly turned the key in the ignition. *Had the music really been this loud?!!!* I fumbled for the off button on the stereo. Next, gently shifting the car into drive, I turned on my signal to merge with the non-existent oncoming traffic, and slowly moved out onto the road. The officer followed closely at the same speed (53 on our cruise control) shortly before finally passing with a friendly wave and disappearing into the night. My imagination pictured them laughing their asses off, getting a kick out of the scare they put into them good-ol' boys from California.

Now we were alone. The car remained totally quiet except for the humming of the engine and possibly my labored attempts to breathe normally again. It was the loudest silence I'd ever heard. I waited for the I-told-you-sos to start. None came. I glanced over at Rich, but he looked straight ahead without the smallest twitch or shift in facial expression. At this point, being yelled at or laughed at (or even sworn at) would have been preferable to this muffled self-loathing.

I wondered if Rich was somehow aware of my internal suffering and punishing me with his silence. After all, a negative consequence, no matter how unpleasant, offers some sort of penance to the wrongdoer and releases him from his guilt. By enduring one's upbraiding, one purchases back the freedom to live with a clear conscience. Perhaps as a former Catholic, I mused, Rich understood this concept all too well. Suddenly I was struck by another possibility: maybe Rich was fully aware of my internal suffering and therefore not heaping any more indignity on top of what I was already feeling. By waiting for *me* to apologize, he could allow me to regain my manhood and own up to my stupidity. Giving my best friend in the world the benefit of the doubt, I decided it would have to be me.

"I'm so . . . sorry," I managed, holding the "so" for a full second to emphasize how incapable I was of expressing the true extent of my remorse. The pause before "sorry" was not for dramatic effect, but absolutely necessary to finish the sentence without crying.

I couldn't let myself. I felt pathetic enough already. Crying might also prevent me from hearing his response, which I hoped was coming soon. Wasn't it? Finally out of the silence came the voice I so desperately needed to hear. "It's all right."

The floodgates opened. No, it's not all right I thought as I sobbed uncontrollably. I was an idiot. I didn't deserve his forgiveness. Rich must have seen my tear-stained face shaking side-to-side in a silent no, as after a moment he repeated himself. "It's really all right."

There are moments in life when we struggle mightily to regain our composure, only to realize it's useless. Our cover has been blown; the timid, frightened child at our core has been revealed and there's no way we can possibly deny it. This vulnerability, exposed in the wrong company, could jeopardize our reputation or career, so most of us have learned how to keep it under wraps in public. Ironically then, saving our best face for those who barely know us, we force our family, our lovers, our best friends—those whom we care about and respect the most—to deal with us at our worst. Do we feel safe to break down in front of these loved ones because we understand that they know who we really are and will not judge us for our weakness? Or is it because we love them and want to impress them so much that we break down when we realize we're incapable of being the perfect souls we wish we could be in their presence?

We drove a few miles further east and spent the night at a Motel 6 in Abilene. Not another word about the incident was spoken until I brought it up, and even then it was only discussed in a joking manner. The next day we continued on to New Orleans, a few days later we were off to Florida, and, after more adventures, we were soon flying home again. Years later I was the best man on Rich's wedding day, and I was also at the hospital to congratulate him and his wife on the birth of their first child. Over the years we've had thousands of conversations and shared countless stories—perhaps none more prized than the time we were pulled over at midnight in Texas—in the company of family and friends as well as alone, and in all those renditions, Rich has never once mentioned my crying in the car, focusing rather on my Academy-Award winning apologies to the officer, the gargantuan size of the troopers, and our highly-embellished bravery in surviving the situation.

Much as I love to talk, to laugh, to connect verbally, and to converse, I have to admit that the most important moments which define a friendship—or even one's life—are often those which remain unspoken.

On a more practical level, though, the next time I find myself in a certain southern state, there will be another unspoken thought that will cautiously guide all my actions.

Don't Mess With Texas.

Halloween Hair

by Cynthia Patton

On October 29th my husband marched into Supercuts for his usual $17.00 trim. The same haircut he'd had his entire adult life. He studied himself in the mirror as the scissors flashed and decided he needed a change. A big change.

Michael tipped the hairdresser and walked to Longs Drugs. He paced the aisles and pondered his options. Then he made his purchase, drove home, and tore open three boxes of L'Oreal hair color: light ash blonde, vivid red, and deep auburn brown. He stood at the sink in his blue button-down shirt and attempted to "fix" his haircut with kitchen shears before he streaked the dye through his silver hair. He left the temples untouched "for a natural look."

I walked in the front door, tired after a long commute, and saw Michael in the doorway to our downstairs bathroom. He asked what I thought, like a child showing off artwork. I stared at his acid-trip hair, unable to speak. It was neon, fly away, electric socket hair. It was cartoon character, worst nightmare kind of hair. My first thought was that a rat had chewed on his head. My second thought was that a rat would have done a better job.

The acrid stench of hair dye brought me to my senses. I noticed dark blotches on the pale tile floor and red streaks on the white woodwork and Michael's khaki dress slacks. Terrified to enter the bathroom, I prayed: Dear God, please don't make me live through another remodel.

I launched into a lecture on appropriate activities for the fancy guest bathroom when our impending photo shoot bubbled through my consciousness. We were four months into the adoption approval process and needed an excellent close-up photo to complete our Dear Birthparent letter. Our file was complete; the photographer arrived in three days. What would she think when she saw the spiky, tri-colored mess sitting on preppy Michael's head?

My jacket was half off, hanging from my elbows. I shrugged it back on and grabbed my bag. "Start washing your hair," I ordered before I fled.

I didn't go far; just downtown to Panama Bay Coffee. After an hour of sipping chai and reading yoga magazines, the horror of Michael's hair subsided. My blood pressure was in the normal range and I'd convinced myself it was no big deal, just an unfortunate waste of water. Sure, Michael had an impulsive streak but he wouldn't be stupid enough to use permanent dye. Or would he?

I returned home to find Michael hunched at the top of the stairs in the dark. He clutched a disgruntled cat in his lap. I squinted at his hair and saw it was a uniform shade—a definite improvement for a business consultant. It would be obvious as hell, but how bad could it be? I reached for the light switch.

"Don't," he said near tears. "Just don't."

In the morning I opened my eyes and almost fell out of bed. Michael's hair was a black hole sucking up the light. The unnatural color might have passed as part of an elaborate Halloween costume—a disheveled Count Dracula—but the dye had leaked onto his forehead and ears in odd-colored splotches. It covered his hands, with streaks zigzagging up his arms. Combined with his look of pained remorse, his appearance screamed home dye job gone awry. He looked so awful I forgot to be angry. His purplish-black hair was punishment enough.

Michael explained after I left he realized the streaking had been a mistake. He dyed his hair red, but that looked worse. So he opted for auburn. "I kept adding dye, trying to correct the problem. But nothing worked."

"Hmm, so this is the home dye equivalent of Tammy Faye Baker's mascara."

He cupped his head in his hands and groaned. I reminded him hair grew and he said, "Not fast enough. I have a meeting tomorrow with a senior partner."

I said, "When's the meeting?" As if an extra hour would improve the situation.

Michael stared at himself in an old hand mirror he'd found at the back of one of the bathroom cabinets. "I don't understand why it turned out so dark."

"Probably because you used three times the amount needed. One box was more than enough. Didn't you read the directions?"

"What directions?"

"Good thinking, Betty Crocker. Why bother with useless equipment like the recipe—or gloves."

He stared at his tie-dyed hands and sniffled. "It's not the color on the box. This isn't auburn, it's...." He searched for the word.

"Purple," I said. "Your hair is the color of a bruise."

I went to work while Michael hid at home, a baseball cap pulled low over his brow. He called with a frequency that drew my coworkers' notice. I ignored their stares, but it's tough to feign innocence when your husband's silver hair is the color of used motor oil with the consistency of a broom.

I stared at Michael's photo on my desk and tried to make sense of his behavior. Michael had caused his share of fiascos during our seven-year marriage, but hair dye was out of character for a man who went to Supercuts because he refused to make an appointment. He had nose hair, neck hair, thankfully no back hair. He bit his nails when they needed cutting. His favorite outfit was stained sweatpants and a flannel shirt. He'd cultivated a classic Brooks Brothers look for work, but overall he cared so little for grooming I assumed he was blissfully free of vanity. Yet somehow L'Oreal—that conniving bitch—lured him like a siren singing from the drugstore shelves.

Even more puzzling was the question of motivation. Michael had been gray for over a decade. Silver hair was part of him, like his lanky build and crooked nose. And why the complete lack of discretion? Didn't he understand the unwritten covenant that a midlife dye job must produce a "natural" look? We all knew Ronald Reagan's hair had been chemically processed, but it wasn't a damn freak show.

I sipped my coffee and realized in my shock and confusion I hadn't bothered to ask Michael why. Curious about the inner workings of male vanity, I told my officemate Briggs I needed a man's opinion. Down the hall, Paul, Dirk, and Ellen were seated at their desks. Paul was the only coworker older than me, the closest in age to Michael. I leaned over a pile of paperwork and asked why Michael would dye his hair.

Paul looked stricken. His hair was brown, more or less.

I described Michael's color choices, and the women gasped. Paul cleared his throat. "He's got it bad—classic case of midlife crisis. The only way to preserve his dignity is to shave it off."

The women giggled while Dirk pretended to type. Briggs said, "I don't think Michael's going to look good without his hair."

No one replied. I tried not to picture it. "We're shooting our adoption photo in two days."

Everyone groaned. They've followed my infertility saga like an afternoon soap.

"What about washing it?" said Ellen.

"Already tried that. He even used Clorox bleach."

The women stared, their mouths agape, while Paul looked at his hands. "He's got to do the full monty, shave it off. It's the only way."

I spent the afternoon trying to read a report. Midlife crisis? Now? I stared at the page and felt my carefully banked anger ignite. Couldn't his crisis wait until after the photographer shot her roll of film? I looked at the photos of my infant nephews taped above my computer screen. Did he forget we'd waited six years for a baby of our own?

I flipped a page so hard it tore. Briggs glanced up and laughed. "Look on the bright side, Cynthia. Three boxes of hair dye are way cheaper than a sports car."

I was calling it a day when Dirk stuck his head in the office. "Why not dye Michael's hair back to its normal color? Actresses do it all the time."

Briggs and I stared as if he had just announced the solution to global warming. "Dirk," I said, "you're a genius."

Michael wanted me to contact my hair salon but I insisted he make the call. I was too embarrassed to explain what he'd done. Later he told me Suzy was a real professional. "She asked about the brand of dye and which color I used first. She didn't have the necessary chemicals, but she found a salon that did. Guess I should have gone to her in the first place."

I bit my tongue. "How did she fit you in so quickly?"

"She said I had a 'hair emergency.'"

Talk about understatement.

I was in a better mood next morning. "Happy Halloween," I said as Michael stumbled out of bed. "Want me to fetch your satin cape?"

"Very funny." He shot me a sour look and headed for the bathroom.

Cold water forced him out of the shower. His hair remained the color of rotten figs, but the dye was off his skin. "Hey, how'd you do that?"

"I used one of those Scotch Brite pads from the kitchen. You should try it. It made my forehead silky smooth."

The dye had leaked into his brain. That had to be it.

He scratched his stubble. "I need an excuse to cancel my meeting with the senior partner."

"Call in sick. Tell him you don't want what you've got to spread." I laughed so hard I choked on my coffee.

By the time I reached the office, I was more philosophical. I sat at my desk, weeding through emails, and wondered if the hair salon could achieve magic. I understood Michael's desire to cover his gray. I'd been dying mine for eight years, had started before our wedding because I refused to walk down the aisle with more grays than I could pluck. I dyed it ash brown—a color Suzy insisted wasn't "in." Tell that to my scalp, I said. I maintained the color with appointments every six, then every five weeks. When I looked in the mirror, I saw the hair I'd always known and it was easy to pretend I hadn't aged. But according to Suzy—the only one who knew the truth—I was 40, maybe 50 percent gray in front, slightly less in back. I tried not to think about it, but the truth was I had salt-and-pepper hair, the kind of hair my grandmother had when she died at 83, the kind of hair my mother would soon have. That was the part that depressed me. No woman should out-gray her mother.

On her most recent visit to California, my younger sister Kris told me she had discovered her first gray hair. Her voice shook with disgust. I patted her arm in mock sympathy and reminded her that I plucked pesky strays in college and had dyed for years. My sister-in-law

Jenny spun around to look at me. No way, she said. I leaned over and smoothed my hair away from the part, exposing the white roots. "Oh," she said, clearly stunned. "I never would have guessed."

That's how I wanted to keep it. I envied women like Briggs who grayed gracefully, or ones like Johanna who dyed for years and then stopped—revealing gloriously silver hair. But I was hoping to adopt a child, and in my dreams I wasn't rocking an infant to sleep with ratty gray hair. I didn't plan to be like Cher, with a teenager's hair tacked onto a 60+ body (okay, bad example). I just wanted to look like a parent when I finally received my child.

When I arrived home from work, Michael was barbequing in the backyard. "The trick-or-treaters arrive in an hour," he yelled. "Get the candy ready."

"How'd it go at the salon?" I was afraid to walk outside, unsure what I would find.

He walked in the back door. "You tell me."

I gasped. Michael was now a strawberry blonde, his hair carefully styled. He was clean shaven, and I caught a whiff of something unfamiliar, perhaps gel or hair spray. That alone would have been startling, but before me stood a younger version of Michael I'd never known.

He ran his hand through his curls and grinned. "You like it?" He danced a little jig. "I love it."

We stared at each other until the chicken flared up.

Between waves of trick-or-treaters Michael told me he spent five hours at the salon. Not one but two women worked to repair his hair. They served him sparkling water with lime and gave him a manicure while they stripped the dye and put new color in. "After two days with that horrible mess I begged for gray hair. I totally begged. Christine told me it was impossible because after the dye was removed my hair would be yellow…"

As in straw.

"… so they streaked it. It's a lighter shade of my natural color."

"What did they say when they got an eyeful of your Count Dracula hair?"

"Nothing. These gals were professionals."

Yeah, right. I wondered how much of the five hours they'd spent in a back room cracking up. I dipped my bread in olive oil and kept my voice neutral. "So why'd you do it?"

"Do what?" His face was the picture of innocence.

"Dye your hair, Michael. Why dye your hair three colors?"

"I thought streaking would make it realistic." He grimaced. "Obviously not one of my better decisions."

"Why permanent dye?"

He dipped a piece of bread. "I was like a guy at Home Depot buying a new tool. I went for the strongest hammer money could buy." He patted his sun-kissed locks. "You don't like it?"

"It's fine, but I liked it silver too. You know that, right?"

"Yeah, I know." He picked at his green beans. "It's just..."

When he didn't continue, I reached for his hand. "Honey, we don't need to do it on demand anymore. We could work on being spontaneous. Spend long weekends in Napa or San Francisco. Even try counseling. A midlife crisis isn't the end of the world."

His head jerked up. "What gave you that idea? I'm not having a crisis. I just figured I looked too old."

"You're not old. You're 46."

"Cynthia, we need to attract teenage birthparents. I've got to look like a hip dad. Who'd pick me with silver hair?"

"I would."

The next morning the photographer posed us in front of a bank of camellias. Michael wore a crisp denim shirt while I wore red velvet—clothes selected to pop against the deep green background and appear casually confident. Clothes I hoped said pick us, we're good parents. Michael stood behind and wrapped me in his arms. The smell of pomade made my nose itch, but I didn't need to remind him to smile.

ego at large (again!)
by sandra kay

love.

  genuine love

would rejoice in your happiness. wish your marriage always well.

and so i rest at last!
in my enlightened knowledge

i do not love you.

because last night i prayed she makes you miserable. —and wished you both pure hell.

then stood up on sunday
sighed and said to God

oh, fine! i hope they both live happily frickin' ever after

(which means i love you)   ~amen.

Sweet Man

by Tom Darter

That's what he called me
    when I was a boy.

(Well, to be honest,
    he called me many things:
    Sir T, Teezeeboy,
    and, when I pestered him, things like
    Nuisance, Botheration, and
    Worse Than the Plague.
But the one that echoes most
    through the hallway
    of my memory is
    Sweet Man.)

At the time, it was just a nickname—
    it had no meaning.
But now, four years after his death,
    it really does mean something
    (and not about me).

He said he let Mom raise me, because
    (weighed down by the soul-deep scars
    from his father's beatings)
    he feared his anger would rise,
        and, in imitation,
        he would be violent—
        would do something
        he didn't want to do.

But, I ask you:
    Is there a better way
    to raise your son
    than to name him so?

And now I know that,
    in calling me Sweet Man,
    he mirrored his own, gentle soul.

Whitcomb's Trill

by J.D. Blair

His exploits were legend. There were appearances on Letterman and Leno. He spent an hour with Oprah. Reviewers raved: "His *tremolo* is unsurpassed," trumpeted one. "Never before has the third movement been so fearlessly attempted," crowed another. "Whitcomb was daring and unselfish in his attack," praised another.

For five years Jeremy Whitcomb commanded first chair in the French horn section of the San Francisco Symphony. He received the coveted Heimlich-Brugel award for creative excellence three years running. His horn work was extraordinary, that much was true. Whitcomb took pride in his prowess but his life was a mess on almost every other level. Before the accolades, before the adulation, before the tongue thing, Whitcomb was just another horn player.

Jeremy lived a simple but comfortable life in the City, renting an apartment on the fringes of Pacific Heights, the upscale neighborhood of swells. But his proximity to the high-rent district allowed him no special privileges with the ruling class across the street. There was one fledgling heiress that occasionally gave him a nod when their paths crossed, but Whitcomb saw it as nothing more than a gratuitous gesture . . . much like acknowledging a puppy on the street.

Jeremy had no close friends to speak of and certainly no romantic connections. There was the youngster Kayla, a fiery-haired oboe player. Just out of Julliard, she showed little interest in the horn section. He sensed in her an actual disdain for brass players.

Without close social ties Whitcomb concentrated religiously on his horn and his talent. His gift was an obsession that would eventually pay off in spades. He recalled with clarity the exact place, time, and circumstance that turned his life around. It was October 23rd, Munich.

It was Whitcomb's first tour abroad with the symphony. He was excited to be on tour and his fervor was exhibited in his development of a quadruple tongue technique that allowed him to produce a trill never before experienced by students of the French horn. The movement of his tongue was so swift and tenuous against the mouthpiece that it produced a purr that caught the attention of everyone in the orchestra, including Kayla. The first time Whitcomb tried the new tonguing during the third movement of a Bach Suite, Kayla shot him a glance he hadn't seen before. Where before there was derision, this time there was envy and even lust. To test her reaction Jeremy embellished the trill in the next piece, a *Rondo*. The results were astonishing and unexpected. Following that opening performance in Munich, Whitcomb found Kayla waiting for him at the stage door, the lustful stare still glistening in her blue eyes. He thought it strange that she kept staring at his lips but assumed it was just a quirk, something reed players did. They exchanged niceties. She said she enjoyed his tongue work. Whitcomb returned the compliment even though he thought her oboe presentation was average at best. As they talked, a small group of women gathered, thrusting concert programs at him to autograph. Others questioned him about the new technique. They all stared at his mouth with the same lustful gaze that Kayla had given him. It became very uncomfortable for Whitcomb and he quickly left, but the crowd of women followed, clamoring after him all the way to his hotel.

After that opening night concert, Whitcomb incorporated his quad-tonguing tactic into every piece. When the European tour ended, Whitcomb's tonguing prowess preceded him on his return to the States. His picture appeared on the cover of *Mouthpiece* magazine, featuring an article analyzing the fine technical points of Whitcomb's revolutionary horn attack. Jeremy reveled in his newfound celebrity.

One Saturday afternoon following rehearsal, Jeremy stopped off at the corner grocery to pick up some things. When he got to his apartment building Kayla was sitting on his stoop sucking sensuously on a reed. "I thought maybe we could work on the Bartok together."

Whitcomb put his groceries down and scrambled for his key. "Sure, the Bartok, why not. Can't get too much Bartok."

Once inside, Whitcomb made them tea while Kayla excused herself to the powder room. He prepared his horn, searched for his sheet music and was polishing his mouthpiece when the oboist stepped from the bathroom wearing only that lustful glint he had seen in Munich. Whitcomb dropped the mouthpiece and got his hand stuck in the bell of the horn.

"Play me," whispered Kayla.

"Play you?" stammered Whitcomb, struggling to free his hand.

"I want you to play me the way you played the Bach in Munich. I want to feel the thrill of your trill."

Whitcomb thought he heard bells but it was the clang of his horn as it hit the floor. His hand, free of the horn, went to his lips, which were suddenly very dry. His tongue flicked over them.

Kayla gasped, "My God you are such a tease. Stop this foreplay and play me, please." She threw her naked body on the couch, laid her head back and closed her eyes. "Please, give me the third movement." She began writhing slowly, humming the Bach suite.

My God, Whitcomb thought, seeing her beauty spread out before him—she's a true redhead. He tore at his clothes while she hummed and writhed. He began humming too. Both of them humming, she the reed parts, Whitcomb the horns. He was on her, his lips forming up against hers and the tongue laying back letting the lips provide the *legato* across her mouth, neck, and cleavage.

"Lower, she sighed." Whitcomb dropped his humming down a half octave. She sighed again, "No, you silly goose, down here." She slid her slim hands down her hips to her alabaster thighs and the bright red thatch of pubescence between them. Whitcomb moistened his lips again and began the *andante* between her breasts and over her belly as it rose and fell in perfect meter.

Whitcomb's lips attacked the filament of silky red with an excited *allegro* and Kayla's humming became an aria. His tongue took on a life of its own; Bartok, Bach, Prokofiev, building to a crescendo that broke over Kayla and altered Whitcomb's mundane life forever.

From that day forward Jeremy would never again be alone and would forever be known as the man who created the "Whitcomb Trill." And the fledgling heiress who lived across the street, she became a strong patron of the arts . . . with benefits.

(untitled)
by Ian Ray Armknecht

temperance is the justification for
a mouth filled with glittering jewels!
behold before you a man—natural
and tired—a weary eye transfixed
on the idle sun!
break away and laugh! cruelest
hour a charitable fiend—thou arte
naught but the fire of love.
prosperous youth and erring glee—
the hour of ornate speech
is at hand! let fly the lips of
lovers and ooze forth the
garrulous sweat of enjambed kisses.
silence startles and the moan
prevails. O! happiest dream of mine—
turn me off like the breath of
liars—drive this staunch heart
to madness and dash its carapace
on the rocky shore!
i want to love! no!
i want to love and smile and
feel the same rain as Aphrodite.
take this tongue and send
it off into star and shore alike!

NanoNonFiction

a library's volumes of reference material abridged by one-billionth

by Jason Hambrecht

Auto Repair Manual

Install a check "Check Engine Light" light.

Red Wine Spectator

This wine has flavors of brambleberries, damsons, and ripe fruit, with tastes of cinnamon, earthiness, pepper, sandalwood, and vanilla with a silky, smooth, toasty, velvety warm finish that pairs well with andouille, bratwurst, chorizo, kielbasa, linguiça, mortadella, pancetta, and salami.

Broadway's Faux Tunes

Ass, shit, and balls! Ass, shit, and balls! The only dirty words we sing are ass, shit, and balls—ass, shit, and balls!

Red Wine Participant

Tastes like grape juice; let's order a pepperoni pie.
World War Three (post-modern NanoNonFiction)
Like, Corsica started shit with Sardinia, and 'en Sardinia got in wit' it wit' 'em and—fuck, man, fuck.

Weird A La Carte Japanese Food

Grains look lonely, when you're sashimi. Fishes come off of the rice—when you're sliced. All raw, yeah.

Bumper Sticker Compendium

My favorite public broadcasting station can kick your favorite public broadcasting station's ass.

Genre Nano-Fiction

by Tom Darter

Note: The genre of each nano-fiction is given in italics just above the title.

Cannibalistic, Serial Killer, Horror Nano-Fiction

Cheek

She was juicy enough, but the makeup ruined the flavor.

Pornographic, Rhyming, Magical Realism Nano-Fiction

Bloom-Day

When her heart grew flowers, he plucked.
When his bud gave nectar, she sucked.
When their souls' vines intertwined, they fucked.

New-Age, Numerological, Gastronomic Nano-Fiction

First Course

The second time his third eye saw the four stars aligned in the fifth galaxy, he was at sixes and sevens, and ate nine oysters, which got her attention.

Not Really Kafka, Just Kafka-esque

by David Hardiman

Flies in the buttermilk
Shoo fly shoo!
Flies in the buttermilk
Shoo fly shoo!
Flies in the buttermilk
Shoo fly shoo!
Skip to my Lou my darling

This children's nursery rhyme seemed innocent enough until the flies made a federal case out of it. Few realized then that Flies v. Old MacDonald would become a rigorous litmus test for future Supreme Court nominees. *Offshore Law Review Quarterly* has published a summary of the case, and, with their implied verbal permission, I've reprinted it below:

Case Review: Flies v. Old MacDonald, (9th Cir 2005).

Case Sensitive: yeS.

Issues: Constitutional Law—First Amendment—Right of Assembly. Also Contract Law.

Finding: Ninth Circuit Court holds the "shooing" of flies as constitutional.

Summary of Events: On April 4, 2005 Old MacDonald discovers flies in the [his] buttermilk and repeatedly requests they shoo [leave].

The Law: Several intersecting themes abound here. The flies' Right of Assembly, Old MacDonald's right to unmolested buttermilk, and the public's right to uncontaminated dairy effluvium.

Overview

It has been said the sum of mankind's supremacy is not so much his ability to control nature, but his ability to harmonize with it. To that end it is instructive to study Flies v. Old MacDonald and its precedent-setting decision whereby the court struck down the lawful right of assembly by a lot (as in the sense of an assortment) of unimproved flies.

The case arose when a lot of flies—engaged in the act of being flies—claimed they were forcibly evicted from Old MacDonald's buttermilk without just cause or due notice, and before they had gained sufficient nutriment to continue doing their business as flies. This, they allege, degraded their ability to carry out their mission as flies.

Both parties to the suit stipulated a familiarity with the nursery rhyme *Skip to my Lou my Darling*, where, against the backdrop of a social compact known as the Social Compact, worldly pursuits are merrily presented as irreconcilably opposable. That is, the flies feel justifiably entitled not so much to Old MacDonald's buttermilk *per se*; but to *the* buttermilk or *a lot* (emphasis added) of worldly buttermilk.

Old MacDonald, however, maintains the (his) buttermilk is justly created by his (his) own good labors and should be his (the) to enjoy, free and clear of any encumbrances including those placed on it by flies. "You see," his council argued, "the prosecution's 'one world, one buttermilk' argument just won't fly (no emphasis added). This is not some phantom buttermilk to be toggled on and off at a polemicist's whim, but rather it is hard earned corporeal buttermilk whose cold and wet tactility lends perfect credence to its nowness," they hallucinated.

Old MacDonald verily believed he had a verbal contract with their leader or "Lord of the Flies" whereby they could freely enjoy his rich bounty of barnyard dung if they left his buttermilk unmolested. All evinced perfect performance until April 4, 2005 when, after witnessing the flies in the buttermilk, Old MacDonald felt the verbal contract had been breached. As a remedy to the flies in the buttermilk, he elected to evict them by exclaiming, "Shoo fly, shoo!" He did so with great *emphasis* (emphasis added).

When Old MacDonald apprehended (as in bore witness to) the flies in the buttermilk, one can readily imagine his horror and easily understand his chosen remedy; namely to "shoo fly, shoo." However a semantic disparity arises at this juncture. Are the flies to be treated jointly or severally? Old MacDonald is sending mixed messages. While comprehending "flies" (plural emphasis added) in the buttermilk, his remedy is "shoo fly (singular emphasis added) shoo." This is confusing to say the least. How do you disperse one fly? What can one reasonably expect an assembly of flies to do? And finally, although it has little bearing on this case; why is it the Museum of Tolerance offers free admission to everyone except minorities?

In any event all agreed that: Old MacDonald has a farm. It's in Ohio. And on this farm he has some flies. Still in Ohio. With a buzz, buzz here and some buttermilk there. Here a fly, there a fly, everywhere a fly, fly. Old MacDonald has a farm. It's in Ohio.

Thirty-two years ago, when the case or Nursery Rhyme was first brought to the attention of Mother Goose's court, it was sent back to the Children's Reading Project without comment. Now the staunch Right-to-Buttermilk people have reintroduced it to a friendlier maggot-packed court.

The substance of the case revolves around whether or not the flies, as creatures of nature, have a right to the buttermilk or, from their perspective, whether Old MacDonald has unlimited rights to his buttermilk. They are clearly both desirous of the buttermilk (again, as in the nursery rhyme, worldly pursuits are merrily presented as irreconcilably opposable). Does the higher functioning Old MacDonald (washes behind ears; knows something is backing up when he hears that beeping sound) have complete and unassailable rights to his buttermilk or, as implied in the Social Compact, must he freely share his societal lucre with others in the animal kingdom (see Sheen v. The Chicken Ranch).

By mutual consent we know there are flies in the buttermilk. As to their disposition we are unsure. For example, to what degree are they in the buttermilk? Are they submerged in the buttermilk and hence drowned, thereby rendering impossible the admonishment to "shoo"? Or are they merely resident in the vicinity of the buttermilk? This was a central question rendered moot when Old MacDonald suggested combining the buttermilk and the flies to make butterflies. This matter was referred to Dr. Moreau.

As in the case of Gobbledygook v. Legalese whereby the court couldn't understand either one of them, so to may this case bemuse rather than enlighten. We hereby review Flies v. Old MacDonald in full knowledge that justice isn't so much blind as it has early onset Alzheimer's.

The Flies' Petition:

In arguments before the court, the plaintiff's attorneys presented a solid if unglamorous case contending, among other things that, "They are flies handsomely engaged in the business of being flies, and attending to buttermilk is one of a constellation of activities that flies do. An *a priori* assumption, such as flies will always seek buttermilk; cannot be redressed. For example, gravity does not grant waivers to those who would prefer to be more loosely tethered to Earth. Gravity is relentless and perfect in applying its gravitational force. That's its duty. Jenny Craig clients would love relief from its omnipresent force. It ain't happenin'. Again, the best we can hope to achieve is to harmonize with nature, not to control it. Gravity is as gravity does. Why should we expect anything else from flies?

"From the flies' perspective this is no one's buttermilk, but merely neuter buttermilk they have come upon within the course of conducting their business as flies. In their world they have no possession and therefore recognize no possession in anyone else's world—Old MacDonald's included. Their occupation of the buttermilk is both incidental and central to their flyness. In substance the case is more about Hegelian realities and less about 'shooing.' [Ed Note: At this point the lawyer put down his bong.] We are willing to grant relief to Old MacDonald, but only if separate and equal buttermilk accommodations are provided. And, as we recognize no trans-species contracts, any so-called verbal contract with the Lord of the Flies is null and….that thing where it doesn't count anymore. As vassal flies, if I may wax feudatory, we are determined to maintain our right of assembly by whatever means necessary, although we strongly feel this entire incident is probably a matter for the courts to decide."

Judge's Interjection:

"That's what we're doing here. This is a court. You're in court."

The Flies Petition Cont'd:

"Perfect then. Let me continue. Although like many pests, we flies enjoy the rich wellspring of lactose emolument, we are not flies in the ointment. We are merely flies in the buttermilk. Additionally, any mention of a contract between that fatuous Goldblum, who fancies himself the Lord of the Flies, and Old MacDonald is preposterous. Goldblum has the reasoning power of lint and is *non compos mentis*. He has obviously flown too close to the bug zapper. Moreover he has compound eyes and therefore would've been entering an agreement with 512 separate Old MacDonalds. Clearly the contract is null and . . . that other thing. And finally, although Goldblum is a registered Republican in Broward County, Florida, he speaks for no one but himself.

"In an abstract sense the flies have always found Old MacDonald to be 'most companionable.' More specifically, whenever Old MacDonald was present, they knew he was there. He registered with them and they greatly prefer the warmth and nourishment of a collegial relationship than the chill and decay of an adversarial relationship."

Old MacDonald's Outburst:

"Collegial relationship? They're pestilential flies, not nourishing colleagues damn it! Now git dem the hell out of my buttermilk," ranted a moonshine-fueled Old MacDonald before the bailiff restrained him. [Ed note: In a peculiar twist, high-speed courtroom cameras indicated it was actually the bailiff who ranted and Old MacDonald who restrained him.] [Author's note: Is this case really any more far-fetched than how babies are made? Okay, then—read on]

The Flies Petition Cont'd:

"Now, as to the shooing of my clients: Having established my clients' unalienable right to have assembled in the buttermilk, any form of eviction, be it shooing, swatting, or zapping, is not only contemptible, but illegal as hell. I have reliable moo-say evidence from unimpeachable cows that Old MacDonald's breath reeked of moonshine that fateful Monday."

Judge's Interjection:

"Hold on, counselor. As I'm sure you know, hearsay evidence is inadmissible."

The Flies Petition Cont'd:

"I didn't say it was hearsay evidence. I said it was moo-say evidence. Allow me to continue. We contend that not only was 'shooing' a threat, but it was an imminent threat for it was repeated three times. Each time it was repeated more menacingly than the first. And each time Old MacDonald reset the unacceptable condition and his preferred abatement, as when he ferociously bellowed:

Flies in the buttermilk
Shoo fly shoo!

[Old MacDonald apprehends the flies' status quo vis-à-vis the buttermilk and once again reaffirms his desire to be rid of them:]

Flies in the buttermilk
Shoo fly shoo!!

[As the flies have failed to accede to his primary and secondary admonishments, Old MacDonald restates their imperfect performance and reissues a tertiary, albeit similar, remedy:]

Flies in the buttermilk
Shoo fly shoo!!!

[As in the case of Griswold v. His Mittens where the court found his mittens were left on the radiator too long, Old MacDonald is flummoxed by the unresponsiveness of the flies and, in a spasm of abject disgust, issues his final cryptic statement to a barn full of animals:]

Skip to my Lou my darling.

We are encouraged by Old MacDonald's 'Skip to my Lou my darling' pronouncement and view it as a basis for settlement. Until then we move for immediate dismissal and complete restoration of dung privileges."

Judge's Response:

"You folks brought the case. You can't move for dismissal you idiot. Your clients, however, are free to enjoy the excremental lucre ad infinitum."

The Defense Weighs in: Jurisprudence or Juristupid

"While we would never attempt to abridge, limit or snooker the First Amendment right of assembly, we do draw a bright line between lawful assembly and criminal trespassing. Flies are known irritants whose societal contribution is limited to reminding us just how annoying this world can be; and as such they are entitled to no milk of human kindness—let alone buttermilk. That they are one of God's creations is a non-starter. Let us not forget, Stalin (if you believed his mother) was also one of God's creations and certainly was entitled to nothing but ignominy or, in Southern states, perhaps ignominy and grits.

"The prosecution agrees with the defense that a first amendment matter, namely the right of assembly, is at issue. But we note the first amendment reads 'right of the people to peaceably assemble,' and not the right of the flies to peaceably assemble. We believe the framers' of the constitution meant to conspicuously exclude all non-people from peaceably assembling, especially flies and particularly slaves. God forbid a slave was found in the buttermilk. He wouldn't be shooed. He'd be flogged. Eventually a great Civil War was fought over the issue. We hope the issue of flies in the buttermilk is not as apocalyptic." [Note: Jefferson flirted with an amendment specifically excluding gloom from our shores but abandoned it for want of enforceability. Jefferson's theme was later embodied in the Harold Arlen classic: "Forget Your Troubles, C'mon get Happy."]

The Defense Cont'd:

"Clearly," the defense argued, "Old MacDonald is conveying an unambiguous message—The flies must go! They are an unwanted pestilence whose presence compromises the health of others as well as the salability of the buttermilk. We maintain that no threat was conveyed or implied; merely an *emphatic* (emphasis added) encouragement to 'Shoo, fly, shoo.' Plainly, Old MacDonald's 'shoo' amounted to nothing more than an earnest request for the flies to vacate the compromised dairy product and to relocate away from the buttermilk. When the request was refused our aggrieved client merely advanced towards the buttermilk to investigate the flies' implacability in resisting his entreaties. Again, Old MacDonald is issuing a clarion call—The flies must go! The court will note that no violence of any sort was displayed or manifested. It's not like we were using flypaper or bug zappers. That the flies did disperse was incidental to any act on the part of our client. Grant it, their abandonment of the buttermilk did serve his purposes, although Old MacDonald would've preferred reasoning with them.

"Since the flies obviously recognize the buttermilk as a high value target, shouldn't they recompense Old MacDonald for its use? They say they disavow possession in themselves and others. Do they still feel this way when gorging themselves on someone else's buttermilk? This argument is defective at best and self-serving at worst. After all, flies do have a word for 'unconscionable.' Wheedling maggots! Don't they understand my client is not a husbandmen born to superintend buttermilk? His destiny also involves baling hay and shoveling dung."

Closing Arguments:

Defense: I'm double-parked. Can we get on with this?

Plaintiff: "By creating barriers, whether mechanical (lids) or verbal ('shoo') to being 'in the buttermilk,' you are summarily denying a constellation of rights to an entire order of insects (in this case *diptera*). This cannot stand, for ultimately their freedom is our freedom."

Judge's Response: "Holy Sh*t! What the Kafka are you talking about man? They're flies damn it! Flies I say! Now shoo—the lot of you." He banged his gavel *three times* (emphasis added) and ruled in favor of Old MacDonald.

Next Case: Rock-a-bye Baby v. Broken Bough

Puberty Problems
by Frank Thornburgh

Along about the end of my twelfth year my little wee wee started growing rapidly. It was no longer a miniature dormant thing but bigger with a mind of its own.

Not only was that happening but I was getting pimples.. . . and my voice was changing.

I had an overwhelming desire to do what comes naturally. Although my buddies had a few suggestions, I wanted the real thing.

I knew what my target looked like because six years prior a little girl my age met me in the horse weed jungle near our previous house and we showed each other . . . our "things."

Anyway, my new constant swelling became embarrassing at school and no doubt hindered my education during English class. The teacher was convinced the only way to analyze sentences was to go to the blackboard and show the class what we were made of. I always knew the answers and was anxious to show my knowledge but didn't dare raise my hand, for my new creature was poking straight out uncontrollably.

 I smashed it. I pinched it. I tried to sit on it. But nothing seemed to work. At first I tried to put it under my belt as I shoved my pants down low on my hips, but I hadn't quite got there yet. I even tried to shove it down my right pant leg, hold it there and walk slightly stiff legged to the front of the class. That didn't work either for it still poked out visibly. Finally the best method was to reach in my right pants pocket and press it to my stomach real hard while walking to the blackboard, then remain facing the board while doing sentence analysis . . . left handed. I'm convinced my shyness started right then when the teacher kept saying, "Talk to the class, not the blackboard . . . and take your hand out of your pocket."

My constant desire to pollinate every flower was not quite blinding, for one day on the playground, I noticed Margaret was growing big breasts. I thought, "I know; I'll send her a note using my new secret decoder ring." The next class was a scholarly waste as I frantically spun the ring to each letter making my note telling her what I would like to do. After I got the note finished I realized, how is she going to read the note without a decoder ring? So I turned the note over and explained the code.

Well, Margaret was not impressed. She gave the note to her teacher and I was sent to the principal's office. Mr. Underwood was expecting me. He said, "You again." He was a late-in-life father of one of my buddies, so I thought should I remind him his son Darrell and I are good friends. No, that wouldn't cut any ice with him.

Mr. Underwood pursed his lips and twitched his mouth to stifle a smile while listening to my monologue defense.

I don't know why I even bothered; I was always found guilty. Again I thought, possibly I should remind him I was under the influence of this thing I'm holding in my pocket. No, that wouldn't work either.

Finally he said, "You'll have to get a paddling for this so bend over." Out came the paddle from the desk drawer: *Whack! Whack! Whack!* "Now back to class."

Margaret and I were on unfriendly terms after that. She'd just have to get along without my attention and definitely, no more Valentine cards from me.

Comin' Down the Hill

From Dry Creek Road

by Ethel Mays

They say that you see your life flash before your eyes just before you die. Well, one hot summer day I evidently wasn't supposed to die except almost from extreme terror. Just before I nearly fell out of the door of a car flying around the bend of a backcountry, foothills road, I clearly saw my mother move her left hand into the middle of the steering wheel and then grab me by my collar with her right hand. She pulled me into her side just as the car door came unlatched and swung open. Then, she placed her right hand back on the steering wheel and the next bend in the road shut the door. A favorite thermos had gone out of the car door, but Mama never took her eyes off the road. She was in a hurry. We had to get to the bank before it closed, and we were running a little behind schedule. I sat as close as I could to my mother all the way into town. I wanted to be sure I got there with her, because I wasn't sure if she'd come back to get me if I fell out of the car, and I didn't want to get blamed for making her late if she did come back for me.

Not long after I almost fell out of the car door, we were late getting down the hill from our cabin and Mama and Grandma were fussing because it was hot. Grandma held my little sister while she slept, and I tried to go to sleep in the back seat. It was either that or suffer through carsickness while Mama drove Grandma's '66 Chevy sedan to its limits down Dry Creek Road. There was no moon that night, but we had quite a few stars. They helped light the way ahead of our anemic headlights.

We almost got out to the main county road before running out of gas, but when Cowboy Shack came into view, we had to pull over and plan on sleeping right there for the night. It was probably 9:30. At about 9:45, when we were just about settled in, a car on its way down the hill slowed, and then stopped beside our car. There were three hunting dogs in the back seat, and it was clear to us that these men had been out coon or possum hunting.

Mama assumed they figured we were out of gas. Why else would we be where we were with the lights turned off? She rolled down her window and opened the exchange. She could talk dogs, coon, and possum—whatever subject was at hand. They talked all of it for a few minutes, and then there was the expected lull. "Say," Mama asked, "you wouldn't be going anywhere near towards town, would you?"

The men leaned towards each other and had a sotto voce confab, accompanied by a lot of head nodding and "umhmm-ing." Then the driver leaned forward to speak with Mama directly. "Wal'," he allowed, "Ah reckon we can take y'out t' Society."

Mama nodded and smiled cordially. You would have thought she'd just wrangled an invitation to tea. She turned and told us she'd come back for us in our other car. She had a blue '57 Chevy station wagon and it was fast. I figured I'd be able to sleep for maybe an hour or so before she returned. "I'll be right back," Mama said, and then got out of our car and climbed into the backseat of the other car with the three hunting hounds. Later, she said she didn't know who smelled worse, the hounds or the men.

I ended up sleeping maybe three-quarters of an hour before Mama got back with her car, but when she returned, she had a can of gas. Mama and Grandma drove both cars out of the hills and we were home by midnight.

A couple of weeks later, Mama and I made a daytrip up the hill by ourselves to take fruit and vegetables to a family friend. On the way back down, we were almost to Cowboy Shack when she suddenly pulled the car over. Dry Creek Road doesn't have a line down the middle, but Mama made sure she stopped well on her side of it. "Hmmp," was all she said before getting out of the still-running car and walking back the way we'd come. I got out, too, and ran after her because I wanted to go see what she was going to do. She sure didn't seem worried about the possibility of being hit by a semi or logging truck coming down the road, so neither was I. She walked with confidence and determination, stepped off the road into the weeds, and then bent to pick up the thermos we thought we'd lost a few weeks earlier. It had one small dent in it but other than that, it seemed in good shape so we took it home. Mama told us later that she'd seen a glint in the weeds as we drove by, and wondered if it might be our thermos. The next time we came down the hill from the cabin in the middle of a hot night, we drank cold lemonade from that same thermos.

The Cow and the Mountain Lion

by Ben Jones

There once was a cow who lived on a farm. She spent her nights in a barn and her days in a meadow with a wooden fence around it. In the mornings the People would milk her and then lead her out into the meadow. In the evening they would lead her into the barn again.

She liked being milked, and she liked being led from the barn to the meadow and back again. The meadow and the barn and the fence and herself all belonged to the People, and it was right that they would lead here and there where they wanted her to go. Her days were passed ambling quietly around the meadow, or eating grass, or chewing her cud in the shade, or following the People into the meadow and back into the barn.

In the wooded hills near the farm there lived a mountain lion. She would often walk by the farm and pad softly past the meadow, just outside the fence, and gaze through it curiously. The cow always saw the mountain lion whenever it came. Somehow she always knew when it was near, even though it moved very quietly and was hard to see in the tall grass outside the fence. She always knew where to watch, and eventually she would see it move or twitch or raise its head. And she also knew that the mountain lion had to stay outside the fence, because the fence, the meadow, and herself belonged to the People, and this quiet, stealthy animal could not intrude on their domain. She knew this, that is, until one day the mountain lion suddenly made a swift effortless leap, and was suddenly inside the meadow with her. And then it was walking toward her. How could that happen? What would the People do?

But there were no People there, and she began backing away from the mountain lion. It came closer and closer, and then she felt a new sensation. She was trembling, shaking, and gasping for breath, and suddenly she was running, running away from the intruder. Running! She had never run before. Or maybe, yes, she had run, a long time ago when she was young. It seemed ever so different now, and she felt slow and awkward. Back then she had run for fun, for joy. This was quite different. The mountain lion followed her, and she knew she could never outrun it, and there was no place to escape. So, she did the only thing left. She stopped and turned around, ready to face it. The animal stopped too, and looked at her calmly. Was it afraid? The cow stepped forward. The animal did nothing but watch her. She took another step, and then another. She finally started walking toward it steadily. The animal turned around and leapt over the fence, and disappeared into the grass.

She was astonished. When she had seen this animal following her, she had turned and faced it with a strange mix of feelings. She wanted to run away but somehow knew that would not work. Instead, something made her stand and face it. She felt a strange energy in her legs, felt them get ready to lash out and kick in desperation. Her neck felt strange, ready to lower her head and . . . what? To hit the creature with her head? No, not her head, her horns! She had horns! So that was what horns were for! She was getting ready to fight, and she had weapons to fight with! To fight, to defend herself!

But the animal had walked away. She would not have to fight after all. It was fleeing! So she followed it in a slow-motion chase, ready to kick, ready to butt. The animal had run away, but for a long time she could still tell exactly where it was.

What amazing new feelings she had. She had run, she had turned and prepared to fight, she had chased the mountain lion, and had driven it off. She had won! She looked and looked into the tall grass, knowing that it was gone but still excited about her victory, and ready for it to return. She ran, this time for joy, around and around the meadow, along the fence. She kicked the fence with her front hooves and her hind hooves and butted it with her horns, over and over. And she knew suddenly, this meadow was her meadow. It didn't belong to the People, it belonged to her! And she could defend it.

As the mountain lion returned to her mountain, she thought about the animal she had played with. She had jumped the fence because she was curious about this big, slow thing that she had seen so many times. She hadn't been hungry, but had wondered how it would act if she came near. Could she chase it? Could she kill it if she wanted to? It was far larger than the deer in the forest, and the deer were both fast and dangerous. They could kick hard, and their antlers could hurt. This thing, though, looked soft and it ran away very slowly. She could smell its fear as she trotted placidly behind it. She had been wondering whether someday, if she ever needed to, she could make a few meals out of it. When it looked back at her and saw her chasing it, and stopped and turned around, she stopped too. When the thing walked toward her, she walked casually to the fence and lightly jumped over it. The thing was sluggish. It could never get over the fence. And it was heavy. If it stepped on her it would hurt. With her curiosity satisfied, she went calmly on her way. Yes, if she really needed a meal, there was an easy one here, maybe several.

The People finally arrived, caught the cow's halter and petted her and rubbed her, but they had a hard time calming her down. She kept watching the grass, wanting to chase the mountain lion again. She could defend her own meadow!

The People became excited when they saw the marks that the mountain lion had left in the soft dirt near the fence. They led her firmly away in spite of her efforts to watch and defend her meadow. She kept looking through the fence and watching the tall grass. Eventually they got her into the barn, and she was not allowed out again, even though she kicked and butted the door until she was tired. Days came and went, and still the doors did not open in spite of her best kicking and butting. But finally they did open, and she ran out into the meadow. There was no need for the People to lead her there. She ran out ahead of them. But there was no sign of the strange animal. Instead, there was a sharp, unpleasant odor along the fence, and she saw a new line of fence posts, with thin wires stretched between them, a few feet outside the old fence. She could hear a faint crackling sound, every now and then, coming from the wires. She didn't like it, but there was nothing she could do but watch for the animal.

After many days the sharp odor and the crackling noise became familiar and she stopped being bothered by it, but she didn't see the mountain lion again, not for a long, long time.

The days of cold and wet had come twice before the mountain lion decided to go to the farm again. She didn't like the new harsh odor that came from the meadow. But now she needed food, and now she wasn't alone. Now she had her three children with her, and they were almost full grown. Feeding them had been hard work. The rabbits and deer had become scarce and careful. Hunting was hard, and they had to range farther and farther from the den to find food. But she remembered that large, slow, clumsy animal. It would provide a large meal for her and all of her children. It was time to claim those meals waiting at the farm.

The cow knew when the mountain lion came back. She didn't know how she knew, she just knew. And she knew just where it was, over in the tall grass, just there. When it raised its head and looked at her, she was looking right back at it.

After many, many days of circling the meadow and kicking the fence, and butting it, and looking through it at the tall grass, the cow was feeling much stronger and much faster. She no longer thought she was made to stand still and eat, and chew her cud, and be led between the barn and the meadow. She was made to defend herself and her meadow, and she was ready to do that. When the mountain lion raised its head, she started butting and kicking the fence so hard that it started coming apart. So she kicked and butted even harder, and soon she had broken a rail, and then another and then a third, and suddenly there was a hole in the fence. She charged out through it, and immediately hit the newer, more delicate fence outside. That had hurt a lot, in a way she had never experienced before, and it startled her so much that she bolted forward with a speed she had never known she had. She was already going so fast that she had already broken through before she could even think about the pain. Then she charged the animal. She almost, but not quite, stepped on it and tried to kick it, but it dodged and jumped out of the way. Then she realized that there were three more like it, right behind. There was one right in front of her, and two on each side. She jumped into the air and would have landed on it with all four hooves if it hadn't jumped out of the way. So she turned to the one on the right, but that one also jumped out of the way. So she turned to the one on the left. She felt ready to give a kick so strong that it seemed like she had been saving it up for this moment. But the animal scrambled out of her way just barely in time to avoid it. She looked around for another one to chase, but only saw four waving tails racing into the grass one after the other, leaving an odor of panic behind them. Suddenly she was alone, trotting fiercely around the battlefield and bellowing victory, and in the distance she could hear the People shouting and running toward her.

When the mountain lion had led her cubs to the farm, the big slow animal had started butting and kicking the fence. She had watched, waiting for an opportunity. When it had finally broken through, she noticed that it was not as slow and clumsy as she remembered. In fact, she had to jump fast to avoid being trampled. But she led the animal back to the children waiting crouched in the grass, with the large animal close behind. She had thought they could all get together to pull it down and kill it. But the animal didn't act like the deer that she had taught them on. This one was acting very strangely, not like a food animal at all. This one was acting like that mouse that had wandered right up to them one day as they rested on a ledge in the sun. It was stumbling and pausing, and even attacked them when it bumped into them. That had made her afraid. It was somehow unfit to eat, in fact it made her want to get away from it, like it was dangerous. So she had jumped up and led her children far away from the sick mouse. And again when that bat had fallen out of a tree near them, and had flailed about on the ground, she had felt the same revulsion and fear, and they had fled. This animal gave her the same feeling, and, in addition, it was very large and very heavy, and was aiming some nasty kicks at her and her children. And it seemed they were feeling the same way, because first one, then another, then the third, and then finally she herself were fleeing at full speed through the grass and into the woods. And they never returned.

The cow never saw a mountain lion again, but still she circled her meadow, defending it. And much later, after another cold and wet time, when she had a daughter, she circled the meadow defending both it and her daughter, and showing her how to defend it too. And when her daughter ran across the meadow, the cow ran along with her, running just for the joy of it.

Saving the Woods

by Bobbie Kinkead

Bertha Digby loved flowers. When she left her parent's home, Bertha brought all the seeds and nuts she could carry. She journeyed to a wide valley and saw a creek meandering through a few shrubs. She flicked her tail and chattered, "The perfect place for a garden." As she dug in her nuts and seeds, she chatted to anyone who listened, "The seeds and nuts will grow into a large woods."

Often she visited her family and cousins in the next valley to bring back more plants. Walnuts, oaks, almonds, alders, willows, elms, fur, spruce, cedars, cherry, plum, and crab apples filled the valley. Flowers, grasses, and shrubs grew in sunny places.

As animals, or birds, or insects passed by Bertha Digby's garden, these folks asked, "Can we live in your woods?" Bertha flicked her tail and cheerfully chattered, "The woods welcome you." She was happy if anyone enjoyed her garden. The beavers built a dam to store the creekwater.

In turn, every animal, bird, fish, lizard, and insect in the valley admired Bertha Digby. These folks knew Bertha cared for every tree, shrub, all the grasses, and flowers. Bertha built an abundant woods for them. The animals were safe. They had food, homes, and their families were happy.

Bertha Digby went on her journey into the next valley visiting her cousins. She wanted more flower seeds to plant under the big trees. While walking home, she saw gray smoke reaching into the sky. She ran up the hill and gasped, "Trees burnt! No flowers!" She saw the animals walking through burned stumps, once her woods. The animals climbed the hill, dazed. They moved with slow heaviness, faces saddened. Bertha Digby ran to them. "What happened?"

The animals weren't sure. Mother Rabbit told her.

"After the bright flash and the loud *boom!*, a gigantic fire blazed fast, high, and hot. The flames scorched us as we hopped for Beavers' pond. The fire blazed around us, burning. We breathed in the thick, dark smoke choking and coughing. Days went by before the smoke cleared, then just ashes! All the trees, all the flowers, our homes, and all foods are gone. The fire ate everything. Many families and friends are missing."

Sorrow overwhelmed everyone. In silence, the animals looked at Bertha Digby. "We are moving to the next valley." They walked to the top of the hill to leave.

Bertha Digby followed them, "There are some trees left. You can build new homes. Stay and help me replant." The animals whimpered from sad hearts, "We move to the next valley."

"There is nothing here."

"The fire ate everything."

"Our families are broken."

Bertha begged on her knees.

They shook their heads. "No!"

Bertha held onto them. "Everyone is needed to replant our woods." She pulled at them, "Our homes will be rebuilt. We will have enough food. Stay, don't go, please help me."

"No, we travel to the next valley." They pushed her away.

Bertha's sorrow burst into tears. "Go, if you want. I will rebuild the woods."

Papa Rabbit hopped over to Bertha. "I and my children will stay. The work will help us with our grief." Mama Bear came over. "The woods are all I know. I will stay with my cubs and help." Mom Beaver turned. "Of course, my family will stay and fix the damn." Dad Beaver added, "With the water we can grow new trees." Hearing Dad Beaver's words about water convinced the others. "The woods was their home and they could replant it."

Bertha Digby took a deep sigh and twitched her tail. "Each cousin will have a job. The work will be hard." She waited.

The animals nodded their heads in agreement. "We are ready to work."

Coyote, Fox, and Wolf dug the dirt while Pig rutted and mixed in the ashes.

The Cousin Rats and Chipmunks carried the oak, walnut, maple, hazel nuts, and pine, blue spruce, fur, and cedar cones from the neighboring valleys. The Cousin Squirrels dug the nuts and cones into the soil.

Mama Bear and her cubs buried raspberries, blackberries, wild strawberries, and currents.

Dad and Mom Beaver with their children repaired the logs in the damn to catch the creek's water.

When Papa Rabbit hopped along with the grass seeds, he tripped and Wind blew the seeds all over. His children gathered flower seeds and threw them to Wind, who again blew the seeds everywhere. All the folks danced and sang.

Birds came and scratched the seeds into the softly prepared soil.

Gopher, Mole, and Prairie Dog dug tunnels to spread the water over the valley for the new tree and flower sprouts.

Porcupine, Skunk, and Weasel protected the new plantings from clumsy feet or hungry helpers.

While the flowers bloomed, Bees, Moths, and Ants spread pollen from flower to flower—growing more seeds for a bigger garden.

Bertha Digby chattered directions and twisted her tail up and down with pleasure. "This is good." "Plant right here." "Enough soil." "More water."

The rain fell with just the right shower every day.

The sun shone perfectly warm for the new plants.

Other folks who lived in the next valleys heard about the planting of the burnt woods. These folks traveled to watch and brought more seeds and trees to plant. Many stayed. The valley blossomed with life and with families pleased with their woods.

One day Dad Beaver pounded a warning, "People come to the valley." Birds hid in the shrubs, insects in the stones, squirrels in the trees, the rabbits in grasses, and the lizards under large rocks. Carefully the people walked through the woods, smiling, laughing, enjoying the growing trees. They smelled the flowers. Bertha chattered to them, "Be careful! This is our home! We love that tree! Easy with that flower! Watch where you go."

Days later Dad Beaver pounded another warning. "People come with long sticks." They worked for days wedging paths through the trees. Bertha chattered to them. "Not here, not there." "Watch the flowers!" "Look out for that small tree." "That's a home!"

After the paths were built, strangers walked through the fresh woods. They talked and laughed pointing to this tree, or that tree, or those shrubs. They touched and smelled the flowers. They pointed at Bertha Digby, who greeted the strangers with, "Enjoy our woods." Then she flipped her tail and chatted out her warnings, "Stay on the paths." "Step carefully!" "That is Beetle's house." "Careful with that new tree. Watch those branches!" "Just smell the flowers!" "Talk softly, new babies sleep!"

The strangers listened and respected Bertha Digby's rules and directions as did the animals, birds, lizards, and insects. The woods grew into a large forest.

To this day Bertha Digby plants trees and flowers while chattering all her rules to strangers visiting her forest.

When Rocks Offer Comfort
(For S. Niedermayer)
by Ethel Mays

When rocks
On a hidden shore
Offer comfort softer
Than the battle fought
A warrior contemplates
The ultimate prize
Of quietude
Loaned with musings
From a mountain
By the inland sea

Armor
Weapons set aside
Mute witnesses to
Bare feet
Departing
    Imprinting
        Disappearing
Into icy water's clarity
And shock

Taut nerves
Remember
Brief unravelings from
Eons ago and submit
To the warm
Rush of hard-won victory's
Golden glow

For a moment

Irish Twins
by Kelly Pollard

The Stick…

Smooth and smaller than a number two pencil. Plastic and foam. I have obsessed over the knowledge contained within this pregnancy gauge. I have held many of these in my hands, crouched in my tiny-tiled bathroom and in the sterile, Mervyn's bathroom stall. Each meeting with the stick was cloaked in different expectations, wavering emotions, and uncertainty.

Our first meeting was Labor Day weekend, over four years ago. I overindulged in the open bar at a family wedding. I glanced at the calendar, at the absence of blood in my panties. I knew something had shifted inside. That wedding reception was my inner toddler taunting the truth, throwing back glasses of champagne and beer with reckless speed in the face of a possible pregnancy.

I put the trip to the drug store off until that Monday, feeling too sick and sure to make it across town. Emotions were a jumble of hope and terror. Deep down inside, I knew I contained life and I was ecstatic. I was also young, unsure, and scared.

I bought one test. This is the only time that I told my husband of my intentions before I drove to the store. Robbie wore a cautious shield over his undeniable excitement. We both knew this was something we had always wanted. We thought we knew for sure that this was the time in our lives to stumble into parenthood, a naïve team.

The woman at the check out congratulated me as she scanned the test. Did she see something in me that I did not? Since when could checkers comment on my furtive purchases? Back home, I read and reread the detailed list of instructions. It resembled a digital thermometer in shape and the blank window would soon answer the question hanging over my household. Hold stick downward. Drench with urine for precisely five seconds. Wait precisely three minutes for result. I did exactly as it said. Five seconds, flat surface on the bathroom counter, hid in my bedroom with the bathroom door closed exactly three minutes. My husband sat in the kitchen, gazing at the newspaper, trying to read our future. With our time up, I crept back in daring myself to seek out the answers to all. Two deep, bright pink lines answered me.

"But, what does this mean?" I asked my husband, the moist stick in my hand.

"We're pregnant." We embraced and laughed and had no idea what was coming our way in nine months, how the cozy dynamics of our two-person household would jolt into crooked paths of uncertainty.

Irish Twins...

"How exciting! Irish twins for the family." My mom was so giddy she couldn't keep her hands still. I watched the veins ripple as she gesticulated to emphasize her curious phrase. Irish twins.

"What?" First trimester exhaustion slowed my body along with all logical thought. Where had I heard the phrase before?

"Oh, you know. Since you're having the babies so close together." She grabbed her checkbook from her overloaded purse and picked an old piece of gum off of it. I entertained the idea of her writing me a huge check for successfully producing another grandchild to spoil. Instead, she flipped to the calendar. "Due November first. That would make them eighteen months apart."

"Irish twins?" I prodded, sipping my diet soda and savoring the small daily allowance of caffeine.

"Like your dad's side of the family, how close in age he is with his brothers. Irish Catholics don't believe in birth control. Hence the big families and close siblings. Irish twins."

"Ah."

Boys, Boys, Boys...

Boys rule my world.

While dashing to the store for an emergency supply of diapers and milk, I faced that catchy phrase on a bumper sticker in front of me. The girl in the white Jetta sang along with Britney Spears while swiping berry red lipstick across her lips. I watched her from behind at the signal light and lost myself in her world, despite the Cheerios flying at me from the backseat and the screeches drowning out the last notes of "Toxic." Next to her, my minivan looked dingy. And me, so much dingier. I used to be that girl, giggling by the lockers because Johnny Quarterback looked my way. Now, I exist on a completely different plane with that bumper sticker the rickety bridge connecting us, because boys rule my world too.

I learned my fate the day that the ultrasound technician swept the gooey film of gel up and over my skyscraper of a belly. I waited for the news, or at least the confirmation of news I thought I had all figured out. I took it for granted that my second baby would be as healthy as my first son. This doctor's visit wasn't about checking for all the body parts and organs configured in just the right way, at least not for me. It was purely superficial.

"And it looks like you've got a little boy in there," the technician concluded.

"Oh." Tears leaked out of the corners of my eyes, carving roads into my pregnancy-chubby cheeks. Robbie squeezed my hand, relieved that, boy or girl, the baby was healthy.

In true hormonal fashion, I cried the whole way home.

"He's healthy," my way too level-headed husband said. Sure. He was thrilled that we had another boy to build on his miniature hockey team, to take on annual backpacking trips and fishing adventures.

My voice wavered every time I shared the news.

"It's a . . . " I'd pause with a deep breath to collect myself, " . . . another boy."

Sniffle.

"That's great, Kel. Bobby will have a little bro!"

Silence.

"Kelly? I thought that's what you wanted."

I did want another boy. I really did. That is, until I fell in love. With a girl name. And as I repeated her name to myself during those emotional first months of pregnancy, I fell in love with her, too.

Hana would have wavy blond hair and her daddy's blue eyes. Japanese for flower and Arabic for happiness, Hana embodied the magic and beauty of what I expected my little girl to be. She would sing lullabies to her massive collection of dolls and host tea parties for her stuffed animals. Hana wouldn't body-slam her poor, unsuspecting dog or insist that a pick ax is really a toy she should be allowed to play with. She'd have pig tails instead of a film of dirt adorning her head.

Each time I repeated the news, Hana faded further from my grip until she was a mere glimmer on an unreachable horizon. I almost resigned myself to the sentence of a life ruled by boys. Almost. Because deep down, I didn't believe that ultrasound. I went along with the routine of sorting through Bobby's outgrown clothes with pictures of trucks and tractors, superheroes and dinosaurs. I spent hours analyzing that ultrasound, convincing myself that the blur between Hana's legs was just that: a blur.

Hadn't the technician said: "It looks like a boy"?

Not, "It is."

Even through the lightening quick labor, when I shouldn't have had time to think, let alone obsess, I expected to meet Hana. When the baby came squalling out of me, I glanced at its face and immediately looked between its legs.

All boy.

Now, two years later, my home is a haze of broken hot wheels, mismatched train sets, and muddy shoes. The music of my life consists of Tonka trucks scraping across cement. My house is doomed to smell like rancid sports equipment and sweaty feet. Sometimes I fantasize about the land of pedicures and princess parties, where the only acceptable toys don't need wheels attached to them.

Boys, boys, boys.

Yet...

Can there be a softer touch than brushing my lips over Bobby's freshly buzzed hair? My hand always stopped my husband's clipper wielding hand when he tried to shave off Shane's blond hair. I still couldn't let go of Hana with her blond curls, so I called Shane my long-haired hippy to disguise that buried desire for a little girl of my own. Only when his hair tangled beyond my control in the regular bathtub thrashings did I succumb. I took the clippers to his head. My tears fell onto the heap of blond wisps across my kitchen floor. He's really just a boy. My boy.

Is this one woman big enough for two mamas' boys latched onto each leg? Is my heart strong enough to crack open not once, but twice, when my sons introduce me to the women who will steal their hearts away?

Why did I have two boys?

I can't even open the newspaper without one of them ripping it from my hands and tearing it apart, all the while cackling with manic delight. It's like they have some sort of speaker wired into their brain that repeats the mantra: *destroy, destroy, destroy.*

And if I do have the chance for a moment of peace with my newspaper and coffee, I smooth out the crinkles in the paper and piece back together the tears. Then my gut lurches as I am faced with headlines about the world falling apart and tallies of lives lost in one war, while other wars threaten to start across the globe. We are trapped in a frightening world of terrorists dropping bombs and poison, with our president shipping thousands of our men into that same abyss of war and terror. Mother Nature cries her dismay with shakes, swells, and swirls of earth, water, and wind. Lives lost, mostly boys. Someone else's boys.

Please don't let my boys grow up wanting to be heroes, don't let them fall into a cause they don't understand. Don't let the government choose for them, whether they will be drafted or not.

Let my boys stay obsessed instead with wheels and dirt. Keep them latched to my legs until they are too heavy for me to carry. I'll take the extra gray hairs, the sleepless nights, the inevitable trips to the ER for stitches, the broken windows, and the rocks shoved into the VCR. And while their father takes them on those male bonding trips around campfires and fishing boats, I will lounge in my silent house with a cocktail and indulge in chick flicks and nail polish to recharge my inner Hana. This one exhausted, outnumbered mom will survive in the end of all this masculine-fueled chaos.

Just, please . . .

Let these boys keep ruling my world.

Juice...

I have moments that define the whole essence of my life. Moments such as this.. . .

A standoff between me and Bobby, both of us bull headed Tauruses. Over juice. He wants it. I want him to take a nap. Juice amps him up and milk winds him down into a sleeping toy. I tell him no. He persists. I give him a cup of milk. He throws it on the floor and declares, "I don't like milk."

I tell him after nap time. He starts to cry. I ignore him. He screams at levels endangering his little brother's nap. I tell him to stop. He screams and cries more. I close my book. Then he forgets for a moment and is absorbed back into his Lion King movie. I open my book up once again.

He remembers. He starts screaming louder. He starts to cough and gag. I slam my book. He continues to scream. An everyday battle. And I give in because I am close to the edge. Any mother knows that ledge of which I speak. The one that if you fall from, you are in danger . . . of yelling, of screaming, of doing the regrettable. It is only a fucking glass of juice, I justify to myself as I slam the refrigerator door. I spill the juice because I am pouring it too fast. I curse under my breath. I toss it to my son without thinking. It pelts him in the head. He starts to scream again. Fuck!

I stifle guilty tears. I hug his angry red body to my chest and breathe deeply. He chugs his juice and I go back to my book. The telltale last slurp. He wants more. I tell him no. The screams return. Smoke feels like it leaks out of my eyes, ears, nostrils, and chest. He continues. I slam the book. This is supposed to be my one quiet, sane moment of the day when the family rests. I get up slowly, tell him Mommy is going in time out. I step into the office and shut the door. I breathe and write and breathe some more until the haze of smoke clears from my eyes and life seems doable once again. I hear whimpers from the couch but he doesn't resort to banging on the door like he usually does. This is the essence of my life. It is only juice.

Space...

Mothering falls on mountains and valleys. Extreme highs of rigor and challenge followed by a flat, bearable pace where the sun will hopefully make an appearance and restore calm once again. I think I hit a slim valley once, maybe for a week last October. Then I adjust my climbing gear once more and make my way up the slope. Perhaps it was never a valley, but a mere ledge for me to catch my breath before the steep incline of life would take over once again.

Looking down from the high plane, one must revel in the beautiful chaos of the journey, take a deep breath, and brag that it was never as bad as we made it out to be while life was reeling out before us. When Shane was still fresh out of my body, and there were invisible magnets latching him to my breast in hourly increments, it had to have been easier than this moment in space. This moment where I am the sippy cup barista, where Starbucks would owe me a raise with all the overtime I put in if I was on their payroll. I am the woman behind the counter, shouting:

"One grande whole milk in green sippy cup."
"One venti skim milk in Spongebob cup with straw."
"One small orange juice with three parts water."
"One tall apple juice with one part water."
"One pot of tar like coffee with a straw, for the barista."

Space is all around us. Why is it we never notice it until we give it up? The space your own children take crosses all dimensions, from the toys scattering your house to the love and confusion that is splattered in your heart, and the wonder and frustration throbbing simultaneously in your head. The amount your psyche is taxed with each child released from within. Your own soul's mirror is in microscopic proportions slowly toddling away from your body.

Space is freedom. Loneliness battles to take over. Usually the loneliness wins out and you decide you need a soul mate to fill it. Then together, you eventually decide that you need a combination of your two souls to place in that spare room, in that vacant backseat. Then the space dwindles and there is love, smothering and sure.

You think you have reached the crest of the mountain, then sure enough, the fog parts and there is another, rockier slope to scale.

Space matters because it overwhelms this household. It is what I lack around my body, when two balls of love and endless siphons of attention hang from each leg. Where I am never truly alone; even when they are towns away, their presence hangs over me, judges my actions and impulses, fuels my passion and love for life, weighs on my liberty and puts a tailspin on my dreams. My pulse quickens when my older one blatantly defies me, refusing to bend to my will. He is separate from me, where once he was housed in the folds of my curving body. He's a rebellious spirit, my soul fleeing from me. The little one clings to my body in the darkest hours of the night, the rhythm of my heartbeat still a flickering memory he refuses to let go of.

My life is now measured in diapers and how many gallons of milk sit in the fridge. A healthy supply ensures no last minute runs to the grocery store with cranky toddlers half past their naps.

My boys, my Irish twins, don't overtake their father. They don't crowd him or weigh on him because they were never included in his body's house. It is always me me me, want Mama to do it, need Mama to tuck me in, have Mommy rock me to sleep, make Mommy line up the Hot Wheels, link the train tracks, roll the ball, stitch the heart.

Mothering is ambivalence bottled inside. It is complete, incestuous infatuation with your soul carried on chubby legs and belly cackles. It is a line drawn, that you can't help crossing when you've reached your limit of patience and have given your heart away. Exhaustion and empowerment. It is dreams realized but never how you expect.

    I live for those shimmery moments when I want to eradicate the space between my boys and my body, want to gather them inside me again and protect them and hold on to them with my love. Many days I need the space to roll out of me an endless red carpet where I can retreat back into myself and stop giving and giving myself, my labor, my love over to them every waking moment, every dreaming moment. Will this draining passion always overtake me long after they've outgrown toddling and have really started living?

    They are my air to live through and suffocate in. They are the twin towers of my own personal plight for meaning. I find it in the hazel flecks of their eyes, the bubble-gum pink of their gums, the ivory smoothness of their teeth, and the twin moles buried under their hair. These Irish, bright-eyed lads are my sustenance.

Mary and the Divine One
by Jennifer Lock

Fish were swimming in the pool
of sweat under her breasts
Her bra had become an aquarium

She was on trial for murdering God
The courtroom could smell
that her alibi was a lie
testimony fell from her lips
shattering on the marble floor

Juror #9 could taste the eucalyptus lotion
she had smeared on herself
Her lawyer said it was
Aromatherapy

She could feel the eyes
of the TV viewers safe at home
judging her, ripping her apart
with their Trailer Park logic

Mary had been caught in Las Vegas
She was no killer of theology
She was having an affair
with mythology
Her plan was to leave
Vegas for Albuquerque
to meet her Lover
during the magical hour
of purple
Making love in the mountains
with the cactus and scorpions

Love isn't always soft
it pricks you, stings you
kills you slowly

She is desperate to take off her
Come Fuck Me heels
Why does it suddenly feel so uncomfortable
to be in a mini skirt and push up bra?

She stood up in the middle of her testimony
and did a strip tease
This is the way she has always
earned her freedom

"Thou Art Forgiven!"
boomed the Voice of Reason
"It's really him," gasped the crowd

Swooping Mary into His arms
planting a kiss on her lips
transporting them out of the
courthouse to become celebrities

Taking the show on the road
Mary and the Divine One
Live in L.A., New York and on Larry King
movie deals and recording contracts

"Whoever said God was dead?" read
the headlines nationwide

Having grown disillusioned with fame
Mary broke it off with God
She walked away from it all
to become a monk
Where each day she meditates on her
reflection in a humming bird's stare

Lunch With Kitty

by Susan Mayall

Sarah is getting dressed for the expedition. It takes a long time. Her body is so bloated now, after all the chemo, that she finds it hard to bend over. Several times she nearly falls off her chair, leaning forward to pull on socks and shoes.

I know better than to offer help. She's fiercely independent, and tries to keep up her normal tasks. "Ch—rist!" she groans, then giggles as she straightens for a moment and pats her belly. "It's almost like being pregnant again!"

But of course it's not. Sarah loved being pregnant, loved small babies, and loves them still when they become teenagers. Like Kitty, the fifteen year old we're going to visit. Kitty is spending a year at an "afterschool," a Danish boarding school designed for children of rural families. It's not far away from her parents' Jutland farmhouse, and I, the visiting aunt from America, am being taken to see her. It's been decided that we'll arrive at noon, in time for lunch with the school, but the way things are going, we may not make it.

Sarah hauls herself up, opens a drawer. "What do you think—should I wear my wig or a scarf?"

I hesitate. I know she hates her wig—it makes her head itch, and besides she despises anything fake. But we're going to be with a crowd of teenagers, and wouldn't Kitty like her mother to look somewhat normal? It's too late to say anything now, though. Sarah has already picked out a long blue scarf and is winding it round her head, so that the short silky fringe dangles over her forehead. With her flushed, puffy face and bulky body in shapeless purple and black she looks quite extraordinary. In a sudden pang I remember my tall, slim sister, her long blonde hair. But she doesn't seem sad, or worried about her appearance. She's excited—she's on her way to her beautiful daughter, and she wants to show her to me. It's an extra special day, in a time when all days have to be special.

Her husband Jorgen drives us to the school. It's an unusually beautiful autumn day, big clouds racing across the sky, sunlight heightening the subdued colors of the Danish countryside. Sarah sighs. "It's almost more beautiful . . . " she says. She doesn't finish the sentence. Often now she can't find the words. She has told me haltingly that soon she won't be able to talk. Jorgen once said that it took Sarah an hour to walk down their little village street. She had to talk to everyone. And when we'd visited Holland together we'd talked so hard we'd almost fallen into a canal. I try to find something to talk about now, and wish we could go on driving. A school lunch isn't something to look forward to, and I wonder how Kitty will feel about having us there.

What I mean is how will she feel about Sarah. Won't she be embarrassed, a fifteen year old surrounded by her friends, to have such a strange looking mother? Not that I would blame her for it if she was—it would surely only be normal teenage behavior. But I dread seeing Kitty's discomfort, Sarah's disappointment—I fear being there. And on top of everything, we're late.

Nobody is around when we crunch up the gravel driveway. There are steps to negotiate before we reach the open front door. Jorgen and I hold each of Sarah's arms, but even so she stumbles, nearly falls, and sits down on the top step. She often feels faint—her children have become used to watching her as she cooks so they can catch her before she collapses. But soon she's up again, and we make our slow progress towards the babble of voices and the smell of institutional food that means the dining room.

At the door, we stop. I feel out of place and awkward. But Sarah is beaming. Down the center aisle, through the tables full of chattering kids who turn to see what she's doing, comes Kitty. Tall, leggy, like a little colt, as her mother once said, she dashes towards us, arms outstretched, her beautiful, wide-eyed face ablaze with love. She flings her arms around her mother, takes her by the hand and leads her to a seat.

And I, abandoned awhile, eyes blurred with tears, feel uplifted, ashamed of my doubts. It is indeed a special day. And I'm privileged, lucky to share a school lunch with people who know how to live, whatever life's imperfections.

blog spot

by sandra kay

Couldn't Resist (me!) sandra, ttgp (shesayswithasmile.blogspot.com 12/21/06) so went today to get a fresh coat of paint. this is the only time i indulge my senses inside the pages of men's health magazine because . . . well, it's there. and i have to do something for 45 minutes. —so i'm flipping through real slow like, looking at all these healthy, fit, tan young male creatures in nothing but their sexy underwear and it is so obvious that their bodies are very real and not airbrushed; those bare rippled stomachs and strong, defined muscular arms, full lips, bedroom eyes, run-your-fingers-through-my-hair-and-dare-me jaw lines.

and don't tell, but i couldn't resist. there was no way i could remember on my own, and no pencil or pad of paper around. so real quiet. real calm and cool like. when no one was looking or paying any attention, i tugged just a little, and very gently on this one page. and before i had a chance to change my mind, wouldn't you just know, the whole page came out of the magazine, practically by itself! it tore so easily and quietly, it was like it wanted to come out. i swear.

and is it really stealing or considered property damage when my goals are this altruistic? and as you will see they really are.

ironically, on page 45, there is a stupid advertisement that reads: turn the page. nothing to see here.

and what a lie, because on the next page there *is* something to see—kinda. it's a digital image of a naked lady (and as usual she's been decapitated on account of your limited imaginations) and in white text with a red background (dec issue/2006) it reads: a woman is far less likely to reach orgasm during a one night stand than with a long-term partner. and her frequency of orgasm is at its highest in the second year of a relationship. this my friends, is what i call an emergency! 9 fuckin' 11.

who has two years? you could die, like, right now reading this . . . there is no time to waste!

then i read on: it says, how she likes it: the more exclusive attention she gets, the more likely she'll reach orgasm. (oh, who is the editor here?!? we don't need attention —we need vibrations!)

and then, most importantly, this! the journal of sex research report card. now pay attention here. i'm copying directly from the page that accidentally fell out of the magazine.

techniques/percentage of women who reach orgasm.

manual and oral stimulation/90%

manual and oral stimulation, and vaginal intercourse/86%

manual stimulation only/79%

oral stimulation and vaginal intercourse/73%

manual stimulation and vaginal intercourse/71%

vaginal intercourse only/50%

—now—i notice two things right away when i scan this

1) there is no 100%

2) there is no mention of a vibrator

and i'm suggesting (or arguing, depending on my mood) that there just might be what research scientists, lawyers, doctors and bloggers refer to as a correlation.

why settle for 90% when you can achieve 100?

and women . . . why on earth would you waste two precious, irretrievable years? orgasms are very important to your over-all health and well-being. they knock apples right off the chart.

you don't need a long-term relationship or manual stimulation . . .

just an outlet and a long cord.

and then, watch how we increase those stats during what will no doubt be a very very happy, healthy new year :)

"gears!"

Why Do Men Go to Strip Clubs? on oprah (or: couldn' resist part II /shesayswithasmile.blogspot.com 12/30/06)

monday, jan 1st, 2007 (!), oprah will repeat a show i've seen before. i plan to dvr it so i can springboard off a quote. seems i remember oprah asking the question of a young pretty brunette girl, "should men feel threatened by vibrators?" and the girl answered, "yes" because they can do things guys can't (or something like that/i want to capture it verbatim).

and i remember thinking . . . what a shame. vibrators aren't a threat— they're a helpful, friendly tool. not intended to replace men; but aid them. and i'm not going to put words in stephen covey's book, (i'll blog them instead) but if he were to write, say, the 7 habits of highly effective lovers, i'm thinking he might a) encourage (not discourage) beginning with the orgasm in mind and, maybe, retell the chopping down the tree story/sharpening the saw; although something about refering to a blade seems wrong and dangerous here, so i'll cum up with something new.

let's start w/a basic review of covey's 7 habits:

be proactive (initiate) begin w/the orgasm in mind put first things first (first being her of course)

think win!/win! (not when?/when?!?)

seek first to please/then to be pleased

synergise! (creative cooperation)

and number 7—sharpen the saw—which i will rewrite in sincere jest as plug in your vibrator.

and now direct from his book w/my earnest editing:

#1 national bestseller, the 7 habits of highly effective lovers, written by stephen covey/edited for self-serving & altruistic purposes by (me!), sandra, ttgp.

pg 287: suppose you were to cum upon a man working feverishly to bring his girl to orgasm.

"what are you doing?" you ask

"can't you see?" cums the impatient reply. "i'm turning her on. i'm going to make her have an orgasm"

"you look exhausted!" you exclaim. "how long have you been at it?"

"over five hours," he returns, "and i'm beat! this is hard work."

"well, why don't you take a break for a few minutes and plug in this vibrator?" you inquire. "i'm sure it would go a lot faster."

"i don't have time to plug in the vibrator," the man says emphatically. "i'm too busy fucking."

habit 7 is taking time to plug in that vibrator. it surrounds the other habits on the seven habit paradigm because it is the habit that makes the ultimate pleasure possible.

habit 7 is personal pc. it's preserving and enhancing the greatest asset of all—orgasms. it's renewing the four dimensions of your nature—physical, spiritual, mental, and social/emotional.

and next week/after i watch the show:

editing appendix a. possible perceptions flowing out of various centers

~shesayswithagreatbigsmile

stay tuned.

Dear My Favorite Blogger Friends. (from shesayswithasmile.blogspot.com 4/6/07)
as you have all decided to take the day off. fine! i will carry the weight today and tell you a story from just the other day. but not yesterday. or the day before.

it all started last month, or last week, when my favorite-of-all-time-use-it-everyday backpack chair collapsed. and please just let me skip right over reliving the humiliation of having my whole body, so suddenly and unexpecedly go crashing—butt first—into the ground.

the long walk from my truck, the slick one-handed unsnap, unfold, and waa-laa!placement of my backpack chair on the grass in the very middle of the very public park beneath the spotlight of the sun. the two-handed, but still slick, opening and first sip of a brand new full-to-the-top cold pepsi i so excitedly placed in the darling fabric cup holder before attempting to sit down...

well anyway.. i bought this wonderful (stupid!) backpack chair last summer at sports chalet. big sign, big red font, said: On sale! Only $29.99! and i fell for it.

would later see the exact same chair at walgreens being sold at full retail price for $19.99.

that kind of thing just pisses me off.

but, oh! how i love my backpack chair! take it with me everywhere i go. so light and portable and comfortable and wonderful in every way. if i divided how many times i've used it by the price i paid. which i would never do because i hate math. i'm sure even at $29.99, it's a real bargain.

so my heart broke when the chair broke and i went racing to walgreens right away for a replacement.

no backpack chairs. none. just those plasticky beach chairs that pinch your skin, or the butterfly kind impossible to get in and out of if you're over 30 pounds.

so to sports chalet i drove!

"got any backpack chairs?"

"in the camping section" he pointed

i ran towards the tents and coolers and there they were: a whole stack of beautiful, wonderful, light weight, portable, backpack chairs with the darling attached cupholders. fantastic! black or blue and for a mere $39.99.

$39.99?!? holy shit. what a rip off! why you'd have to love this backpack chair an awful lot and use it everyday to pay a stupid price like that!

and so i went to the register carrying my new backpack chair—on my back.

and this is where it gets a little tricky.

out of, like—nowhere—or the star trek enterprise, a handsome man is beamed into line behind me. he speaks to me, says, "how much is the chair, it will save me having to walk back and find out."

and i—having just read the price: $39.99. having been pissed off at the $39.99 price. having just gone over, and worse, standing directly in front of the register where i just paid $39.99!

—forgot the price.

and let me here please just skip over the part where i said to him . . . or to be more accurate, where i kind of asked, "$29? no . . . it was more than last year, but less than walgreens . . . $40?

no that doesn't sound right.. i paid more than last year, i know that for sure! well, duh . . . let me look at my receipt." meanwhile the price is practically blinking on the cash register in front of me. but, no, i unzipped my little mesh purse, pulled out the receipt i had *just* put in, and hope i eventually said, $39.99. i can't be sure.

then i went to my truck. my car? i'm still not sure what to call it..

but instead of driving off. i find myself stalking. i mean, stalling. —*stal-ling*—i just sit there a minute, looking around, recovering from my three-hundredith-million embarrassing episode. la, la, la, la, la.. hum diddy doe . . . and then watch as he walks out. and i just happen to notice . . . he did not go to a car in the parking lot, he headed to the bookstore.

and so, it was then, hit me like lightning and i realized—this is my one and only chance before my trip next year to get a new cd!

and so coincidentally, i found myself right behind him in the bookstore.

and i went back to the music section . . . started looking for kelly clarkson's "respect" -she did an awesome job on this remake . . . but it's nowhere on the back of her cd's, this song..

so i went to the computer to do some (oh! there he is! eye contact! big smile) research and found out kelly doesn't sing respect on her cd's, but it is on the american idol greatest hits, which is not in store and needs to be ordered.

and so i went straight then (where did he go?) to jason mraz. and since my daughter permanently borrowed the two jason mraz cd's i used to have . . . i decided to get two more. $18.99 each.

—$18.99?!? holy shit. i had no idea! it was not in my budget; no way.

and so i walked to the counter, paid $41.30 for mr. a-z and waiting for my rocket to come.

went to my car. opened up, popped in my new cd, opened the sunroof and drove home singin' *all about them words.*

over numbers, unencumbered numbered word
hundreds of pages . . . pages, pages forward
more words
then i had ever heard
and i
feel
so alive!...

Fred Rover, Dread Rover (by (me!) sandra, ttgp shesayswithasmile.blogspot.com 6/2/07) car show at the fairgrounds behind me, plus the farmer's market ahead . . . my neighborhood is packed with people today; mostly men. they're everywhere!

this would have been the perfect day for me to discover Fred Rover One in my garage, but no. the streets were practically abandoned that day; some three days ago now. i was so alone.
and terrified.
there i was, all showered, shined and good smellin, in my cute tea length denim skirt, white shirt and sandals, with the bare skin of my feet, and darling red painted toenails all vulnerable to the outside elements
i grabbed the silver metal handle of the garage door, gave it a secret code combination twist and then started liftin'
and i was smiling. i was smiling because i knew once i lifted the garage door all the way open, which requires me toward the end to balance on my tip-toes
i was going to be rewarded with the beautiful vision of all the hard work i had put into cleaning, vacuuming and organizing my side of the garage.
"wow! you truly are amazing sandra" i thought to myself, "and brave!" —because it is scary, scary, scary moving boxes all around when you just know in any given second a big, fast, creepy, crawly thing and all its cousins are going to come racing toward you. but i wore gloves and i had spray
plus james morrison
so got the job done.
and didn't i just feel all proud of myself as i was hopping in my hybrid to take off for the day. i removed my right sandal (because otherwise i can't work the gas pedal), reversed her out of my beautiful clean garage onto the driveway and put her back in park so i could hop out and pull the garage door closed
and that's when i saw him
that's when i screamed and did the heebie-jeebie dance; one foot bare
there he lay on his back, in creepy crawling motion, on a freshly sprayed and vacuumed, perfectly clean patch of cement.
is this the devil at recess; or God at work?
and i know that most people when meeting neighbors for the first time, might say something like, "hi. my name is blah, blah, blah . . . what's your's? and, nice to meet you and things like that
but i spotted a lady minding her own business on the other side of the street and i felt quite comfortable yelling in a panic
"hey!—you know anything about bugs?!"
and that's how i met my three doors down and across the street neighbor laurie. she came over just like that and took a look. and she debated out loud whether he was a cockroach, or a beetle, or some other bug creature that starts with a p . . . parlimeeto? —can't remember.

some bug that loves wood—which—as an artist, i just happen to have three shit loads of in my garage

but she said . . . "i get them too. you can just sweep them out and the birds will eat 'em."

too late for that, though. i already poisoned natures bird food.

and me being who i am, i had to take his picture. because i'm planning on graduating from my own mental academic bug desensitization program.

i tapped into my courage reserves just to scoot that stupid quarter next to him and help tame my own exaggerations about how big he was. without that quater, which took me some ten minutes plus to sweep near his frozen dead, poisoned body, i would have claimed he was the size of a hub cap on an airplane's tire

but i think this effort, as pathetic as it is, qualifies me for entry level hope status in the college of that's enough!

but now i must confess, when i uploaded his pictures on my computer, clicked slide show and portraits of Fred Rover One—unidentified dead bug on back, flashed full screen size on my monitor screen

the only twelve steps i took were instant and backwards.

"holy to God shit!" i screamed. jumped out of my chair, covered my face, ran backwards into the wall and started singin' opera.

it is a genuine full-fledged phobia.

and after our photo shoot, Fred Rover One remained on the floor, quarter next to him, because, for one, i just couldn't tolerate being near him again, and two, i had to show him to my children.

they love this kind of thing: mommy scared shitless.

and they delighted in telling all about the giant bug in our garage to the crossing guard on our way to school. then she started talking to us in great detail about these cockroach, beetle like creatures, some 5 inches long, she used to get at her place in florida. "they fly" she said. and quite instantly i jumped back and gasped at the terrifying image she put in my mind of this thing in my garage flying at me.

my children just laughed and laughed. —but having heard this, didn't i consider it a gift from God now that i found Fred on the ground. on his back. immobile and helpless.

had i gone closer to Fred with the toxic spray can, and he suddenly flipped over and took flight toward me . . . i promise you i would still be running around pleasanton with one shoe on, one shoe off, waving my arms wildly in the air yelling "code orange! code orange! somebody call 911!"

and this brings me exactly where i hoped to eventually arrive. at eric kandel's work with sweet aplysia, the marine snail, and the difference between habitization and sensitization.

i understand the results of his research completely, but struggle like heck trying to explain it to others.. . . . the threshold . . . that tipping point . . . but here i go again:

habitization goes like this: i see Fred. i run and scream. —but— through repeated exposures to Fred, eventually, over time, i go from a run to a walk, from a scream to a sigh, until one day, even the sight of six giant Freds floating in my cereal bowl doesn't phase me.

this can also be referred to as a miracle.

sensitization goes like this: Fred attacks me. i run and scream. end up in the hospital with a bleeding ulcer. someone wants to help through habituating me; thinks by showing me a thumbnail size picture of a Fred in a calm environment, i'll slowly recover

but instead i have a heart attack and die.

it is crucial, crucial, crucial -life or death- to understand the physical/mental impact of that initial stimuli so you know whether desensitization techniques will hurt or heal.

and now, yesterday, i encountered Dread Rover Two, fred's not-lost-long-enough-for-me younger brother.

i ran for the spray and sent another early bird for just a worm.

but i think i might hide the spray and prop the broom against the wall where i can see it and get to it quickly.

then next time i encounter one of these Dread Rovers in my garage

i'll hop on and fly away.

Grant Theft Auto ((me!) sandra, ttgp shesayswithasmile.blogspot.com 6/25/07 under the influence of skinny's post & comments: http://myrant-skinnylittleblonde.blogspot.com/sentencing/june 23rd)

red; stop. green; go.

that was the extent of my knowledge when i put $1.98 in the tank of my boyfriend's car at rotten robbies gas station across from the high school.

i was a freshman. —on the days i attended.

and terrible, typical, me: his car was blue. that's all i remember. it was the envy of many boys on campus, and my boyfriend was very proud of whatever make and model it was, but to me, it was just my boyfriend's blue car.

"thanks for letting me borrow your . . . " —he cut me off. gave me that look.

"oh! almost forgot! i mean, thank you for letting me steal your car."

and then he smiled with approval. gave me his keys and a kiss.

because, that's how we rehearsed it:

"if . . . if, if, if you get pulled over for any reason," he told me,

"just tell the police officer that you stole the keys out of my locker"

the logic here, according to my genius boyfriend and my very best friend, sue-sue—both older than me and with much more experience, was that *if* i got pulled over, and *if* i told them my boyfriend gave me the keys . . . he would go to jail for contributing to a minor, or something like that . . .

but *if* i got pulled over, and *if* i said i stole the keys from my boyfriends locker . . . well, then . . . that's only joy-riding.

—i might get off with just a warning and my boyfriend sees no trouble at all.

red; stop.

green; go.

that was the extent of my knowledge. so when the light turned green: i went. next thing ya know, i'm waking to the sound of some guy's finger's snapping "are you awake? can you hear me? how many fingers am i holding up?"

and thank you to this very day, and this very experience i'm certain, that should i live to be 100 years old, suffering from cancer, dementia and alzheimer's combined i will, no matter what, still rise from my hospital bed, open my eyes, pull out the tubes and put in my teeth to mouth the words "yield right of way" when any guests, visitors or hospital staff ask me about making left turns on green.

now, seems to me, once the snappy-finger ambulance guy assessed that i was alive and well, and that the tennis ball size lump on my forehead was not life threatening, he escorted me to the back of a police car and said goodbye.

and i remember two policemen in that car. one driving. one in the passenger seat. both of them looking back and forth at each other and smiling.

"how old are you?" the driver asked.

and it took me a minute to figure it out. whether i should tell the truth or not.

"14." i answered.

"and whose car was that?"

and that's when everything came back to me in an instant. the whole script. just like we'd rehearsed.

"that's my boyfriend's car. he's a junior. i stole the keys from his locker. he doesn't know i know the combination to his locker. but i do. he would never, never, give me the keys to his car. no sir. or the combination to his locker. i figured out the number code and stole his keys. i wanted to take his car for a joy-ride . . . "

and i do remember quite vividly—even now—how those cops looked back and forth at each other and smiled serious smiles.

then, the passenger-policeman picked up his radio and called the station

"this is.. (blah, blah, officer number, blah, blah, blah) , we've got a (insert special code number here) in progress. we're bringing in a sandra for booking

(for booking!?!? oh shit!? —*No script!*—*Not rehearsed!*)

and then the police officer in the driver's seat glanced back at me and asked —do you know what we're booking you for?"

"joy-riding?" i choked out in a hopeful whisper while i massaged the tumor growing on my head

"nope." he said, "grand theft auto."

"grand theft auto?!?!" i screamed in a panic.

"do you want to change your story?" the passenger police officer asked me, "or, do you want to stick to that story about how you figured out the pad lock combination and stole the key's from your boyfriend's locker?"

what a fix!

—meanwhile-—sue-sue, my best friend, partner in crime, and how-to-get-out-of-jail-free consultant, is . . . to the rescue!

i don't remember the details, except, she was driving in her car (legally, i might add) on the same street i was joy-riding on . . had to pull over to the right when a couple police cars passed her by, and then pull over again for the ambulance and bein' the older and experienced best friend she was, she thought the worst right away. drove further down the road and had it all confirmed.

she looked from a distance to see if i was okay. —she'd a' been arrested had she gone any closer, with those unpaid tickets and fines she accumulated and once she saw that i was okay . . . saw me —me!— in the back of a paddy wagon she raced to the mall, parked, then ran to the store where my boyfriend worked.

in her retelling of the story, she hit him over the head with her purse because he asked about his car before asking about me and meanwhile i'm bein' held in the local slammer for grand. theft. auto.

now, i won't have this exactly correct, verbatim, or anything, but next thing i do remember quite clearly, is that i was allowed to make that one call. and as i sat there with this golden opportunity before me, i recalled my mother's words —my mother's mantra really—"if you ever end up in jail, don't call me!"

this was my mom's version of tough love. she had watched her brothers and all their closest friends end up in jail. call mom. post bail. get out. go back. repeat. repeat. repeat.

she was gonna nip juvenile delinquency in the don't-bother-calling-me- belt-spanked-bud.

and so i didn't jump at the chance to make a call. and it seems to me, some new police officer entered in on the scene. started threatening me with real jail time. "not just a holding room at the station," he would tell me. "a jail cell!"

and i remember, quite vividly, thinking to myself *"please! please! please! please!*—send me to jail. send me to prison!" 'cuz a jail cell, even one surrounded with hardened criminals, would be less punishment than what awaited if i called home.

home.

where an abusive, severely alcoholic step dad would be more than happy to teach me a lesson! and now, i have no memory of making that one call.

no memory of how i ended up back at home.

no memory of what happened, ultimately, to my boyfriend's blue car; except that it was totalled.

vague memory of having to . . . pay a fine? take a test? do community service? appear in court?—before i could get my license two years later at age sweet 16.

but a very vivid memory of my step-dad yelling that because of my stupid selfishness, we'd all end up broke and homeless.

the car that should have had the right of way on that green light was not a car at all, but an animal control truck. a government owned vehicle.

"You were in the wrong! Driving without a license! You stupid Idiot! You hit an animal control truck—do you know what that means?!? They're going to sue us! They will sue us! Someone is going to come here and take this house away, your mom will be without a house! They'll take us for everythying we've got and more! We'll be living in the street—and do you know why?!? Because of you! What made you think you could drive a car? You idiot! Idiot! Selfish Bitch! I ouughta beat the living shit out of you. Go ahead! Sleep on that bed. They'll take that, too! Evertying your mom and I have ever worked for will be gone because of you! I oughta beat the living shit out of you! You'll wish you had died in that accident!"

and he was right. i wished i had died.

—thought about how peaceful that might be; being dead.

—thought about how i didn't deserve, really, to be here on earth.

—thought about what a selfish, stupid, person i was. what a huge disappointment. what a cost. what a burden.

—thought about my mom, brother, sister living in a cardboard box because of me.

—thought about my boyfriend having to walk to school or ride his bike, or hitchhike and get killed because of me.

decided maybe, everyone would be better off without someone like me ruining their hard-earned lives.

my mom would later come in my room and forgive me. comfort me. express love and concern over anger and hatred. probably her, and her alone, or her plus God, saved me from a clearly planned out, visualized and accessible overdose.

so in the end, the car was totalled; the charges were dropped

i stayed alive.

me and my boyfriend with the blue car broke up.

my mom and alcoholic step-dad divorced.

no animals, nor the driver in the truck were injured.
fines were paid.
lessons were learned.
always,
to be continued.

Monoblogue
by David Collins

I've never been a therapy writer. You know, somebody who thinks their childhood would make gripping reading. I mean, I'd be willing to put my seventeen years in mediocrity boot camp up against anyone's on the first installment of Survivor—Childhood if it gave me a crack at a million dollars, but my growing up is only interesting to me, and yours is only interesting to you, and come to think of it, the same goes for jobs and marriage and your medical history. They're fine to learn from, but they're not fascinating stories in and of themselves simply because we won't tell the truth about ourselves. We can't stand it. Even if we knew it, unlikely as that is, we couldn't stand to put it out there.

We don't have so much trouble being the innocent victim while we shine that light on Uncle Phil's philandering or Aunt Oprah's drinking, but in the story of the trek westward that is our clueless start in life, we all leave ourselves at the end, standing shiny clean, like Tom Sawyer's aunt had gotten after our souls with a bucket of cold water and a towel like a file. No weakness, no shame exposed, no fumbling for the zipper to hide our adolescence because our hands never got close to it in the first place, at least not in any story I'm likely to share with you, or you with me.

There's not enough heat in the entire olly-olly-oxen-free literature of ourselves to even get my hand warm before I try to sneak it under Kelly Linkugel's bra, completely unaware that the bottom hem wasn't going to be all lacy and accessible like the top half, and then letting that iron curtain of sixties whalebone queer me on even thinking about trying again until I was seventeen and it was a different girl, and we were sitting in the front seat of my car, mine, not her mother's 1842 Chevy with a steering wheel the size of the Maginot Line for crissake, and the humiliation had worn off just a little bit, dulled by the knowledge of the size of Darrell Hutyra's penis. You're not going to get the truth of that story out of me.

Besides, it would only remind you of a story you wanted to tell me about when you were thirteen, and that wouldn't have any truth about you in it either, and then we'd be forced to have a glass of wine to toast our collective cowardice.

Internal Blog - Tuesday 9am:

You're standing there, one hand stabbing the air, the other on the knob, the half-open door ready to slam home the first time you say something pithy enough to storm out on, when I'm caught by your eyes, green to hazel depending on your clothing and your mood. Just now they're absolutely emerald and flashing like those spinning, *petit mal*-inducing wheel covers that pimps and realtors put on their H3s to demonstrate just how far taste and money can reside from one another.

I have no idea what you're pissed about, and while I didn't think I wanted to know a minute ago, now I'm intrigued and I wonder what makes your eyes light up like that and could I make it happen whenever I wanted and what would the sex be like, except now you've been going on so long that to say "Hang on a minute. Would you mind starting over? I missed your original point," might seem insensitive, and would probably only send you onto a new and unexplored track into the weakening wilderness that is evidently my character.

Two roads diverge in a yellow wood.

Your free hand is pointing at something over my shoulder which you've probably named already and I'm too snake-charmed to turn and try to figure out what it is. It would break the flow and make you think I'm not paying attention to whatever you're agitating against. So I try to look interested without appearing the least bit amused while my brain scans my memory of the room behind me.

There's the television, of course. Maybe I watch more than you do. I'll admit that. But I never noticed it pissed you off. I did sort of snap at you the other night because you wanted to initiate a light chat at exactly the same time Tech was beating A&M. I mean exactly, like literally at the buzzer, with the ball, Jarrius Jackson, your voice and the sound of the horn all in the air at the same time, so close that the crowd sat there sucking its collective breath until the ref signaled it good. It really wasn't that important to me. I don't care about Texas Tech, or A&M, except that the Aggies are going to the Sweet Sixteen this year, miserable rat bastards, and Texas isn't, and Bobby Knight can kiss my ass win or lose. I don't recall what you said, but you seemed to think I was acting like the game was more important than you, and that wasn't my intention at all.

But maybe it's not the TV.

There's that stupid glass parrot from that little hole in Mexico. I will fix it, I promise. I just don't know where the super glue is.

What else? Plants. Not my problem, except there are too many of them.

The cat. Again, not my problem. I'm actually nice to the cat. I let it in, I let it out. I'm a fucking cat doorman, but I don't rag on you about it.

Kitchen? Laundry? I don't think so. We've been there before, and your voice gets this tired thing when we talk about domesticity. Your eyes don't flash green. And I have the distinct feeling you're talking about some specific thing confined to the living room.

The amount of time I spend on the computer? I'll admit that one too, but it's not like you don't have a Hotmail account and a page on Myspace and a Youtube login, so stay off my case about the computer.

I don't think it was something I said. You'd be pointing at me, not the living room.

Beer cans. That could be it. I moved them from the sill behind the sofa to the bookshelf, just like we agreed, but they stay, dammit. Some of those babies hover between rare and antique. Primo. They don't make that anymore. It was crappy beer, but the can's a collector's item. A steel Schlitz with zero rust. Dixie. Pearl for christ sake. Lyndon Johnson had Pearl shipped to the White House. Acme Gold Label. You can't steal this kind of stuff. And like you don't still have every friggin' piece of paper that you ever touched. Don't talk to me about accumulated junk.

It's probably best if I don't figure this out. If it dawned on me I probably couldn't keep it off my face and you'd think I was about to rise up and engage in the conversation, and you'd just dig in so you wouldn't have to share any of the oxygen. Better to cling to my ignorance and let you run down.

There's the big chair you hate, that you swear you're going to replace but never do. It gives you something to dislike that isn't me.

Got it. It's the collage I got at the street fair from the chick with the big tits. I said it was a 3-D representation of everything that was wrong with self-referential post-modernist abstract expressionism. You snorted in that way you do and said I only bought it because the artist had big tits. You don't know that her business card is still taped to the back, do you?

But it's not the painting. You sneered at me for buying it, not the artwork itself, bad as it really is. Your eyes aren't lighting up like this over crappy art.

What would you do if I stepped over there and kicked the door shut and dragged you into the bedroom, threw you on the bed and told you to shut the hell up. I bet your eyes would be greener than they are right now.

But we'll never know will we? Because we both know I'm not going to do that. It's not my style in this world that you've written me into. Instead, I'm going to stand here in the headlights, stuck in neutral, curious, but passive.

Yet, I really do want to know what's behind me that makes your eyes so green I can't turn around to see for fear of breaking contact and I'm not willing to do that, either.

So I'll risk it and ask. Kind of like asking you for a date all over again. Hedge around it for the longest time, then say fuck it, what'll it cost me I haven't already paid?

But I take a breath and telegraph it, and that's all the response you need to declare victory, and it's at that moment that the half-life of your anger clicks down to nothingness, and you spin around the nucleus of the door and snap it shut behind you like an exclamation point, probably harder than you intended, but not as hard as I thought you would, and I stand there.

I'm strong. I don't look behind me.

I just stand there.

Adam
by Harold Gower

Oh, Stone Age man
You hardly know…
You cannot comprehend
The wonders of the universe
The galaxies as they extend…

Some day you will begin to learn
In thirteen thousand years
That sun and earth and moon are spheres
And how their orbits run.

For now we'll talk in simple terms
That you can understand
We'll speak in terms of day and night
The darkness and the light.

We'll talk about the firmament
The waters and the land
The rivers and the garden
The animals and man.

We'll talk about what you can eat
And what you mustn't try
For now you'll have to just obey
And not to question why.

As you observe the elements
Your reasoning will increase
In thirteen thousand years perhaps
You'll learn to live in peace.

Andy
by Frank Thornburgh

As we walked out of the squad room, Sgt. Runyon asked if I wanted a reservist to ride with me. I didn't like the idea, as some were said to gossip and I preferred to get into trouble on my own. I looked at Andy, noticing he was ten to fifteen years older than me with a care-free aura, so said, "Sure." Out at the car, we did the usual routine of checking all the lights and equipment then got in and started out of the parking lot. I said, "Andy, call us in service." He took the microphone, put it between his legs and passed gas with a long melodious tone. Our female dispatcher said, "You're 10-8 unit 3204." I knew right then we were headed for some wild times together. As it turned out we had five great years together working swing and graveyard shifts while he neared retirement from the navy at Los Alamitos Naval Air Station.

Three other police departments shared our busy radio frequency, so we not only learned to jump in "space available," but also got to know several officers on the other departments by their voices alone. It wasn't many weeks before they knew Andy and I were on the prowl together by the way we went "in service" on the radio at the beginning of our shift. Occasionally a voice came back on the radio, "Hellooo Andy." I never learned to pass gas on command, so it was always up to Andy to radio our unit "in service." Strangely, I never was officially charged or called on the carpet for the way we went "in service," but we sure got reprimanded, suspended and temporarily drummed out of the corps for other things.

Two guys riding patrol together as much as we did talked about everything imaginable. His first navy years were typical rotations of sea duty and shore assignments. After Andy was well acquainted with a lot of the higher up navy brass plus many friends in strategic offices, he got pretty much whatever assignments he wanted which currently happened to be crew chief on the naval-air flight line at Los Alamitos Naval Air Station. All he had to do was put in six more months of easy duty and then retire. He was already interviewing with Douglas Aircraft in Long beach for a job after retirement.

For the next five years every time I was rotated to evening or graveyard shift, Andy frequently rode with me.

Reserve officers were sworn-officers, fairly well trained, but not paid directly. They were technically volunteers. When off-duty job requests for uniformed officers came in, the jobs were first offered to those volunteer reservists. Off-duty pay was pretty good, so it nearly compensated for their reserve officer time. Andy rode with me mainly for the adventure and excitement, for I was a young go-getter, a nonconformist, difficult to supervise, and frequently in wild incidents that I dug up with a lot of hard police work that likely often saved me from being fired. I'm sure I would have been asked to resign if I hadn't set records for recovering so many stolen cars and bagging so many bad guys. The department was also constantly short handed.

Insubordination and off-duty escapades kept me on the edge with the department. Usually Andy was with me when these incidents occurred. The department had a policy that if an officer was officially charged with violating any of the thou-shall-not sections in our secret bible, they were given a choice. The first offense of minor violations varied from one to three days punishment. The choice was extra duty without pay or being drummed out of the corps for the same number of days. When Andy was involved with me, he stuck precisely to our story and stood right beside me when I always chose to be drummed out of the corps. They couldn't do much to Andy except put a letter in his file which he didn't care about. I did the suspension bit mainly for the publicity and the extra days off. Extra days off were nearly impossible any other way. I think I was the only one ever to choose being drummed out instead of extra duty. Everyone else was afraid of losing their jobs or just couldn't afford the loss of pay. I couldn't afford the loss of pay either but did it anyway. (We made $488 a month starting pay.)

Here's what led up to our first suspension. Andy and I had just started swing-shift duty and were patrolling down 17th street when we spotted a '52 Chevy making some minor traffic violation. The car was driven by a good-looking woman; so we decided to stop her to talk. I didn't like to write tickets, but I did stop a lot of violators to talk to them. Since she looked like a real desperate character, we both had to walk up to the car to check out her driver's license and registration. The car didn't belong to her. I checked to see if it was stolen. The report came back, not stolen. She said she was a single parent on her way to work and appeared so. Out of sheer habit, and sorry I did, I ran a record check on her since it wasn't her car. The report came back that there was an outstanding warrant for her for a parking ticket. I told Andy, "I'm not going to arrest a single mom on her way to work for a parking warrant." I told her she better take care of that ticket and the warrant and get on to work.

There are very few secrets at any police department, especially since all radio transmissions are recorded. Later that evening one of the hard-nosed watch commanders called me in to hear my version of what happened. (Remember I was always on the edge.) I just said I was not going to arrest a single mom on her way to work for a measly parking warrant.

The next day I was called into the chief's office with Andy for the "Ceremony." I always harbored a suspicion that everyone, including the chiefs, enjoyed this ritual a little, but never let on. The routine was like this: Andy and I stood side-by-side at attention facing the chief. On each side of the condemned stood the field sergeant and watch commander who were on duty at the time of the violation. The chief then told us that two plain clothes (assholes) from the detective division went out and took the little mother to jail. We were charged with section 3.13.2 of the bible which for the first offense prescribed three days extra duty or suspension. We were asked for our side of the story again and did we choose extra duty or suspension? We always chose suspension. It wasn't quite like the French Foreign Legion, they didn't rip our shoulder patches off but did ceremoniously ask for us to hand over our official I.D. cards, badges, and hat pieces which we had handy for the occasion. We were then told we were no longer members of the department and to report to the city clerk's office in three days to be rehired.

That routine was repeated over and over for:
- Not having my seatbelt fastened.
- Insubordination.
- Not answering the radio, suspected sleeping.
- Shooting a rabid dog. The citizens were not out of hearing range.
- Repeatedly not answering the radio.
- Organizing unauthorized shooting practice on a junk car off duty at our pistol range. (We furnished the car but one of my buddies had on identifiable uniform pants.)
- Trying to break a drunk's neck while being photographed by the media. (He nearly killed a mother and her three kids.) We made a deal during the suspension ceremony involving the chief receiving the photo negatives.
- Constantly failing to answer my phone at home.

There were lots of things Andy and I did without being caught. He had these wonderful binoculars he bought in Japan. Either the coating or the great lenses enabled us to use them like night-vision scopes. Occasionally on graveyard shift we brought our BB Guns to hunt cats with the binoculars.

I didn't engage in Bushwhacking (embarrassing lovers) when patrolling alone, but when Andy was with me we watched them through his binoculars until the crucial moment, then drove up and shined the spotlight on them.

Andy and I just loved to arrest and transport humorous or foul-mouthed drunk drivers, men and women prisoners from bar fights, or any other prisoners with a gift for the unprintable

English language. For these entertainers we jammed the police radio microphone down in the crack of the seat in a way that held the transmitter on. We then drove along for a few minutes entertaining all four cities. Of course, "unintentional" was our story when called on the carpet.

City boundaries were important right down to the inch measurement when it came time to decide who did an accident investigation or a crime report investigation. But police officers from neighboring cities temporarily stood by as a courtesy at borderline accidents and crime scenes, then departed as soon as possible. Barroom fights were different. They were fun. Neighboring cities always volunteered when asked for back up on big fights.

An infamous rowdy bar called Sneaky Pete's sat just on the other side of Westminster Ave. from our city line. About once every month or two Santa Ana had a 415 fight there. Andy and I were nearby during swing shift when Santa Ana put out a call for assistance on a big fight at Sneaky Pete's. We were the first unit to arrive and could hear the fight clear out in the parking lot when we drove up. I shut off the engine, looked at Andy, and said, "I ain't going in there." Andy looked at me grinning and said, "I ain't going in there either." We agreed to wait for the rest of the army, which did arrive shortly with plenty of red lights and sirens. Usually a lot of sirens slowed the fighters down a bit. We let the Santa Ana officers go in first. The fight hadn't slowed down much. Inside, Andy and I got two six-and-a-half foot gorillas separated and started talking to them. On these deals, no one wanted to take anyone to jail unless forced. It was a futile exercise since everyone was guilty of something. One of these two gorillas was ready to quit, but the other guy wanted to try out Andy and me at the same time. We were allowed to do choke holds at that time so one of our other officers walked up behind this dude, put a choke hold on him with a night stick and he was on the floor limp in about five seconds.

Just a week or two later, when I came on duty for swing shift, the talk around the station and at briefing was that two big guys knifed each other to death behind Sneaky Pete's. Apparently, they were both living in a cab-over camper mounted on saw horses behind the bar and got into a knife fight inside the camper where they both bled out. Since it was a couple of days before anyone found these two guys and it was the hottest part of the summer, I sure wasn't in envy of the Santa Ana officers assigned to that case. I got to thinking about the news as I sat through the boring briefing we all had to go through prior to the start of each shift. I was thinking about the recent bar fight Andy and I were involved in at Sneaky Pete's; wondering if there was possibly some connection. During a lull in the briefing I asked if anyone knew where the bodies of the knife-fight guys were. I was informed that they were going to be autopsied at a certain mortuary in my beat. As soon as I hit the streets I went to the mortuary. I knew embalming was done there by medical students. Police officers eventually got to know just about everybody at the hospitals and mortuaries so we had a few privileges. I walked in the back door of the mortuary right into the embalming room where three young guys were working on three bodies. I asked if I could watch for my own education. They said, "Sure." The bodies were two big men and a little girl. The whole scene was creepy. After one glance at the young girl I knew I couldn't watch that one. As I looked at the two men being worked on, I said, "I know these two guys. What are their names?" When the medical technicians told me, I recognized that these were the same two Andy and I had separated during the big fight at Sneaky Pete's. I thought to myself, "Wow, too bad Andy's not here to see this."

Well, as I watched, the technicians started opening a chest cavity with long-handled pruning snips chopping through the ribs. They examined and removed the internal organs and placed them in metal bowls. Next they opened the main veins under each arm and at each crotch to connect little tubes to pump pink fluid through the system until it squirted out one of the other three spots. Laying nearby was a little three inch circular saw they said was used to remove the top of the skull.

The room was summer-hot. The air had a strange heavy smell. The bodies were on special individualized white metal tilt-tables with gutters and drains and running water. I began to get dizzy and light-headed. I asked to be excused to go back outside for fresh air. After a few minutes, I thought, "Maybe Andy shouldn't see this after all." I went back in and told the technicians I'd had enough education for the time being.

The next time Andy rode with me I sure had a lot to tell him, in colorful detail.

The dispatcher sent us to check out someone acting crazy. As I drove up, we saw a young man about twenty years old, six foot four, 250 pounds laying across the sidewalk and curb with his head down in the street. It looked terribly uncomfortable. I asked the kid what he was doing and what was going on. He said, "The people standing around here think I'm crazy." I asked the bystanders what they knew. Then I explained to the kid that people who appear to be a danger to themselves and others have to go to the county hospital mental ward for three days of observations. He agreed he should go so I put my handcuffs on his hands behind his back. His wrists were so big I could only get the cuffs on the first notch or two. On the way to the hospital he decided he didn't want to go. Andy and I kept explaining to him he needed to go. The big guy was trying to kick the windows out and squirming around so I radioed our dispatcher to call the mental ward and have some orderlies meet us to get this kid into the building as Andy and I were not big guys at just five foot ten, 170 pounds. When we pulled into the parking lot, there were people watching us from every window in the two-story building. Andy and I got out, opened the back car door, whereupon our prisoner started kicking his way out and onto his feet doing a pretty good job on Andy and me. I looked toward the hospital for the help, but no one could be seen anywhere. We danced around for a minute in the parking lot until the kid was totally focused on planting his size thirteen shoes into Andy's soft places. I crawled up the guy's back and pulled him over backwards. With his hands cuffed, he couldn't break his fall so his head hit the pavement sounding like a hollow coconut. He was out cold. I told Andy, "Grab his other arm and we'll drag him in." The missing orderlies met us inside the swinging doors so four of us were able to get him on a gurney and strapped down before he woke up. After I took my cuffs off I discovered they were sprung out of alignment and wouldn't work any more. Back at the station I told the watch commander the department should buy some new handcuffs for me. The amazed watch commander gave me his cuffs to finish the shift. The next day the chief called me in and said the department was willing to buy new cuffs for me if I let them keep the bent ones. I made a big mistake and have regretted it ever since. I let them have the rare conversation pieces.

Andy and I suffered and laughed through many other incidents, most of which are deep down in my memory or fortunately forgotten since some should never be told. Other people from that era told me they haven't forgotten us or our escapades.

Five years later and a few weeks after I left the department to go back into aerospace work, I called my estranged wife to ask about our kids. She said, "Did you know Andy was killed a few days ago?" I was immediately shocked and enraged responding, "Why didn't you tell me sooner?" Then I called Andy's house as I knew his phone number as well as my own. His adult son answered the phone and said they just returned from the funeral. Andy was directing traffic in the middle of an intersection during the Strawberry Festival when a driver drove through the intersection while reaching in the back seat. The car hit and killed my friend instantly.

I miss him and think of our wild times together and him standing beside me as we're drummed out of the corps together. I often chuckle to myself when I'm alone reflecting on things. I still clearly see Andy grinning while passing gas into the police radio microphone then the dispatcher says, "You're 10-8 unit 3204."

Frank Rothman

by Harold Gower

You treat me like I don't exist
You turn your head as I approach
Look at the ground or at the sky
Look anywhere but in my eye.

My wife and I live all alone
Our solitary private lives
Each other's warmth is all we need
That's what we tell ourselves indeed

We walk to town you turn your backs
We carry groceries in two sacks
I pay my bills, I do not lie
I do not gossip as I try
To keep my insulated space

Our house is larger than we need
It's largely hidden by the trees
And shrubs we planted years ago
When we were young and I was strong

You called on me to dig the graves
For your illustrious relatives
But now my final debt is due
The tide has turned, I call on you.

Purple Orchids
by Diana Carey

It had been another boring day at work, and Lisa was glad to get off. She hated her job; it was something that required no thought. She did the same boring thing every day, there was no future in it. She had held this job for five years but she could not bring herself to leave. She was afraid of interviewing for another.

On her way home from work that evening Lisa stopped by the store to buy something for dinner and a box of wine as she had run out the night before. She parked her car, got a cart and started going up and down the aisles, just for something to do. She picked up her wine and a frozen dinner. Since she lived alone she rarely ever cooked. It was just too much effort for one person.

As she was walking the aisles she came upon a display of purple orchids. She had always loved orchids, so she picked one up and put it in her cart. Why not take it home and introduce it to the rest of her plants?

When she got home and had finished unloading her car, she took the orchid and placed it on her dinning room table—right in the middle of all the other plants.

"There, now you are home with all your new friends. Don't tell the others, but I think you are the most beautiful."

Lisa went into the kitchen to cook her dinner and pour herself a glass of wine. She did not bother using wine glasses, they didn't hold enough. No, a water glass made it so she didn't have to get up as often. Then she went and put a movie in the DVD to watch while she was eating. She wasn't feeling real light and fluffy tonight, so she decided against the Brendan Fraser movie and settled for *Meet Joe Black*. Sure, the guy dies in the end, but that was how she was feeling tonight.

The next morning she woke and dragged herself out of bed to go to work. She hated getting up in the morning, it seemed like her job was invading her life. Not that she had much of a life. Nobody ever sent her emails, or called her, or sent her a letter, or visited her. She came home from work, locked herself in the house and watched TV most of the time. Of course, she would go out to the store to buy her wine. Not the same store every time. No, she didn't want anyone to think she drank too much, so she went to different stores.

She got dressed and headed out the door.

When she returned home that night she noticed that one of her plants was drooping. She had watered it, so it wasn't dried out; it was just dying for some unknown reason.

Well, I guess plants do that.

She left it there on the table, as throwing it out would take too much effort. She went into the kitchen and poured herself a glass of wine and sat down in the living room to drink it. She didn't feel like eating anything. She had three or four more glasses of wine and went to bed.

She had an even harder time getting up that next day than she normally. Arriving at work fifteen minutes late she slipped in quietly and moved over to her switchboard. Nobody noticed her coming in late. Nobody ever noticed her. It was like she was just part of the furniture. She liked it that way, though. She didn't have to really talk to anyone. Just the people who called in, but all she did with them was ask who they wanted to speak with.

A few days later, her boss, Mrs. Rovai, came in and told her they were going to be putting in an automated phone system the next month and that she was going to have to find something else.

Shit. That's just about right. I know it is because they hate me here. Where am I going to go? I can't get another job.

On her way home that evening Lisa was feeling even more like no one cared about her. It was unfair that they were going to replace her with some technological monster.

They'll find out. That stupid system will get it all wrong and then they'll find out that they really did need me. They'll see.

As Lisa walked into her apartment she looked at her dining room table. Two more of her plants had died.

I can't even keep my plants alive! What good am I?

The next few weeks were about the same. Lisa forced herself to go to work, came home to find another plant dead, then spent the evening drinking her wine. She even stopped watching any movies; she just wasn't interested in anything.

Her last day at work was nothing special. She had no friends so no one took her out to lunch to say good bye. She sat at her switchboard feeling alone and useless.

The next day she stayed in bed until eleven. Then she took her medicine and slowly got up and dressed. She had a glass of wine for breakfast. She didn't have the energy to make anything else.

She went into her computer room and turned on her computer to check for emails. There were three, one was an ad from Borders, another was from some place that sold medicine over the Internet and the third was from an x-rated site. She wondered how they had gotten her email address.

The box of wine was almost empty, but she had another ready to go. She had already opened it so she would not have to worry when she needed it.

Lisa went to sit and read her emails again. She had looked at them now for several hours, but could not remember what any of them said, or if she had replied to them. She didn't think she had, she just didn't feel like having anything to do with other people. Really they were only spam and didn't require a reply anyway.

She got up from her chair and went back out to the kitchen to fill her glass again. Then she sat in front of the computer staring at the screen, thinking.

I am just a waste of space. I can't do anything right and I can't talk with people. Everything I try I fail at. I can't even keep a simple job. Nobody will hire me for a responsible position. Here I am, brain the size of a planet and nobody wants to use it. Why the hell do I bother?

Lisa stumbled out to the kitchen and refilled her glass. She went into the living room where the TV was showing old reruns of *Star Trek*. She sat down for awhile and stared at the TV, not seeing it, as she continued to think.

What the hell am I here for? I'm just a piece of shit anyway. If I mattered to someone it would make a difference, but nobody wants to take the time to get to know me. I'm as good as anyone else. Oh, hell, I know I'm just a piece of shit.

She got up from the couch and walked slowly into the bedroom. She could not see anything around her. She felt like she was in the bottom of a deep well. The sides were dark and there was no light coming in from the top; it was like there was a cover over her. All she could see was what was right in front of her. She made her way over to the bedside table and sat on the bed drinking her wine.

Why am I here, taking up space? What do I matter anyway? No one would know if I just disappeared. I think I will disappear and put myself out of everyone's misery. It's not like anyone would miss me.

She looked at her bedside table and all the bottles of medicine there.

The medical industry might miss me, but not much. There are enough other sick people in the world to keep them rich.

Lisa picked up one of the bottles of pills. It was a prescription she had just had filled, so there were hardly any taken out of the bottle. She walked back out to the kitchen and refilled her glass of wine. Then she went to the living room again to watch *Star Trek*.

She sat on the sofa and, almost without thinking, opened the bottle of pills she had brought out with her. She poured three or four in her hand and popped them in her mouth, washing them down with the wine. Then she took some more, and then more until the pills were gone. She dropped the empty bottle on the table next to her and went into the kitchen to fill her glass again.

On the way back from the kitchen she noticed her orchid sitting on the dining room table. It was surrounded by other plants, but the orchid was the only one still alive. She pulled it out of the pot by the roots and carried it into the living room, dirt falling on the floor.

Lisa sat and stared at the purple flowers she held in her hand. There was something about them that she could not quite understand. She had thought they were so beautiful when she bought them. But she could not remember what beautiful was anymore. Now they looked dark and ugly. The purple was bizarre somehow, not a real flower color.

As she stared at the orchids they started to fade in and out. They were getting darker and darker each time they came into focus.

They are dying. It's what should happen to anything that ugly; it should die.

She continued looking at them, but the flowers seemed to get heavy, she could no longer hold them up. Lisa laid the flowers in her lap. They seemed to move, they were crawling away, off her lap and across the sofa. She just watched, she could no longer move her arms.

As she watched, the flowers turned into faces. Dark purple faces that laughed at her. Ugly, terrifying faces, morbid and cruel.

She could not see anything now. Her eyes would not focus and it became a strain to hold them open. She closed her eyes and felt as if she were floating, nothing was touching her.

Still, in her mind's eye, she could see the purple orchids laughing.

Why I Write, Part II
by Selene Steese

I write to slay my demons
and be reborn from their ashes,
to weave a word rope long enough
and strong enough to help me
scale the stone sides of grief's deep
and endless well. I write

so that when I am lost, I may have hope
of being found. I write to lay
my dead to rest, to remember
the shortness of life and the timelessness
of joy. I write

to deepen in self love, to breathe
more easily, to fit less itchily
into my skin. I write

to scream, to rage against change,
against changelessness, against the indifference
of nature and the brutality of time. I write

to psychoanalyze my life,
dissect every decision,
pick apart any imperfection.
To give Jung and Freud
and Masters and Johnson
and everybody's mother
a run for their money. I write

to give myself a hard time,
and to give a hard time to anyone
who gets in my face. I write

to face myself, to expiate
my sins of self-effacement. I write

to drag myself up from the basement,
from the windowless root cellar
of my soul. I write

to avoid growing old.
Not to stop aging, but to leave behind
responsibility. Sometimes

I avoid writing completely.
Yet even when I don't write
with a pen, my mind writes,
my eyes, my lips, my body
write. I write

because I write, because
I write, because
it's right.

The Journal
by Kathy Mima

The journal had seemed ordinary. Myrtle had picked it up at an old estate sale. It must have belonged to an artist as there were a couple of sketches in it. She'd noticed by a few jagged edges that some of the pages had been torn out. "This will do," she'd told herself and had taken it home to practice drawing in. But she'd never had the chance.

At her apartment the phone had rung telling her about her sister. She'd packed quickly, just a few clothes and her nerve medicine, and she'd thrown in the journal without really thinking.

Now, in the quiet of her sister's secluded home, she picked up the book so she could browse and dream. Myrtle had never had the luxury of being an artist like her sister. A feeling of guilt fluttered through her and stuck in her stomach. She was proud of Opal's accomplishments, of course. The walls of this old house were covered with her paintings and portraits. She liked her sister's style. But Myrtle wondered what might have been had she been allowed to study art and Opal been required to clean houses to support the family.

Myrtle riffled the pages, imagining what the artist might have drawn next on all this blank paper. Something caught her eye; there was a sketch that she hadn't noticed before. It seemed like a face in the midst of several lines, but the eyes were unfinished, giving it a haunting look. It made her think of Opal, lying there in the open casket of which Myrtle hadn't approved, but which her sister had requested.

She felt a little chill and put the book down to crank the window halfway closed. Winter was on its way. The old trees were tall and dense, the woods having crept ever closer over the years. Maybe if there had been children to fight for the yard . . . but there never had been. The leaves were gold and brown, red-tipped like Fall berries. They swirled in small flurries on the ground below.

Reaching for the journal, she chose a blank page and began to doodle. The lines had not yet taken shape when the phone rang. She put down the book and asked, "Hello?"

Silence. The breeze picked up leaves and scattered them against the door like a spidery knocking. Myrtle hung up. "Perhaps they're having trouble with the lines." She went downstairs to put the kettle on for tea. She lit the stove and filled the kettle with water. Drying her hands, she left the towel nearby to remind her not to touch the metal handle. She'd been a bit distracted of late, understandably, and didn't want to burn her hands.

Myrtle had been made responsible for all of Opal's affairs in such a short time. She mused about the rush from her apartment to the airport and the airport to the hospital and the few hours she'd had before her sister was gone.

Opal had said she would look out for Myrtle if she went first and had reminded Myrtle of this while weakly squeezing her hand with those talented, bony fingers. She said she knew that Myrtle was the practical one, the way she'd always worked so hard while first Mama, then Daddy had fallen ill with the fever and passed on. She knew Myrtle had kept the both of them from the orphanage back then, and she told her that soon she would be watching over Myrtle.

Myrtle didn't want her sister to watch over her; it made her nervous to think of dead people, even relatives, watching her from beyond the grave. She thought of her sister's drawn face staring up at her from the hospital bed, and she thought of those hollow eyes in that drawing in the sketchbook. Then Myrtle went upstairs and took some of her nerve medicine.

The journal was lying on the bed, but the page she'd been doodling on had been turned by the breeze. She found herself looking into those eyes again, into that face, and shivered. "I should put this thing away," she muttered, and she moved toward the window to shut it against the evening chill. As she turned the crank, she noted how quickly the sun was setting with all the hills and tall trees around.

It really was beautiful country; few neighbors and lots of nature. Myrtle looked at the walls with Opal's seasonal renditions of the view. "Of course, with time and scenery like that, anyone could—well, anyone with talent, perhaps, or with training—oh, shame on me!" Myrtle felt that stab of jealousy, the spitefulness, and it alarmed her. She'd thought she had let go of her disappointment years ago, but here it was, ugly and smoldering. "Either I put this drawing business out of my mind completely, or I give it a try and see how it goes." She paused. "Well, I suppose I've already tried putting it out of my mind for over fifty years now. And that doesn't seem to be working so well."

Myrtle reached out for the journal again, and thumbing through the pages, she mused, "I wonder if I'm hoping for inspiration." Suddenly she stopped. Frowning, she turned back a couple of pages and peered at the strange lines. "What is this?" She tilted her head. "I don't think I missed that one, but I must have." It was quite similar to the sketch she'd seen before, but this one was more detailed. The lines were beginning to outline a room of some sort. And there was that face, mouth open and eyes still haunting. It looked as if the person was screaming, and she could almost hear the shrillness of it. Myrtle reached for her nerve medicine. "Maybe I'll take just a little more," she told herself. "No use in being frightened."

The wind did have a shrill note to it this evening. It almost sounded like a voice, high-pitched and whining, insistent and—she shuddered. "That really does sound like a scream. No one would be up here, though, this far out of town," she tried to reassure herself. "Perhaps I'm just a little tired." But there it was again, and as she reached to draw back the curtain, her sleeve caught the corner of the book and it dropped to the hardwood floor with a resounding smack!

Myrtle and her heart jumped and turned. Her eyes had just taken in all there was to see outside: trees, trees, and more trees, thick around the tiny dirt yard with its woodpile in the corner near the back steps. Now she found herself staring at the offending object—but what page was this?

She bent down to pick up the open book slowly, seeing what appeared to be a more detailed version of the drawing she had just been looking at. "But I couldn't have missed this." A draft snaked by her legs, and she rose to place the book, open, on the table. Seeing her nerve medicine there, she decided to take some. "I must have forgotten my evening dose," she reminded herself.

Now the creepy sound screamed more incessantly, and Myrtle could feel tiny hairs begin to rise on the back of her neck and arms. "Why—Heavens to Betsy!" She smacked her forehead with her left palm. "What a ninny I am. I left the tea kettle on!"

Before she had time to smile, the telephone rang loudly. She gasped, then partially released her breath and reached a slightly trembling hand for the receiver. Her nerve medicine didn't seem to be helping much tonight. She might need to take a little extra, even though the doctor had told her not to. She lifted the receiver. "Hello?" She waited. "Hello?" She heard nothing on the other end of the line. "Really! I certainly hope it won't be long until they fix these lines." She hung up. It didn't seem windy enough to be causing a serious problem, but this was the country. Maybe squirrels chewed on the lines or something. She felt a little tired and then remembered that she was heading downstairs for something.

Before she moved her heavy feet, however, fluttering pages caught Myrtle's eye. There certainly was a draft in here. She pushed the door almost closed while she placed her fingers on the paper to still its wild dance. The journal's page revealed a more developed line drawing of a room somewhere, somewhere familiar, she sensed. She gazed across the room, pondering. Looking back at the page, the room seemed more detailed, more clear, and—somehow more familiar.

A grating, scraping sound froze Myrtle's hand in the motion of smoothing the page flat. She drew up her courage, though her heart beat like a bird's, and peeked through the curtains to see the wind tousling the trees, their branches scraping at the side of the house. Quivering, she swallowed some of her nerve medicine.

Turning back to the sketchbook, she gasped, realizing that the picture had actually developed more. It seemed there was a face at the window. Myrtle could see it almost glowing as if by firelight. She wondered what magic was this and felt confused and tried to think of a room she'd seen with a fireplace somewhere. The face was terrifying, and Myrtle wanted to close the book but found her fingers riveted to the page. The intense sensation of recognition in her foggy brain forced her to draw every clue forth, grinding it over in her mind. So intent was her stare that she could almost smell the smoke of it; there was a fireplace or a wood-burning stove as it lit up the window frame and cast horrifying shadows around the glowing face. The features were distorted and frantic, and Myrtle realized with terror that there was an arm raised holding something in that eerie glow.

Myrtle could smell the acrid smoke, she could feel the fear, and her eyes grew dry and blurry. She blinked her burning eyelids, burning from being open so wide, trying to fathom the familiarity of the illustration and to solve this desperate puzzle. As her vision cleared, she was shocked to realize that the room looked like the room downstairs and that the window, that window with the horrible face in it was the window at the top of the kitchen door! Was the book trying to warn her somehow?

Myrtle turned and fumbled for the phone to call someone—the sheriff. But the line was dead. She turned back to the drawing, falling against the bed. Even more details—the picture was so vivid. Her nostrils burned with the smoke, and she saw the figure at the door, arm raised and wielding an axe! She clutched at her throat, choking with terror. Myrtle felt dizzy with fear, dizzy with the strangeness of this picture, dizzy with the smoke now pouring up the staircase and filling this room as it had the whole upper portion of the house.

She rose, tearing the page from the book, and yanked open the door. Nearly toppling over from smoke and heat, she turned, but the room had disappeared in the choking cloud. She stumbled and fell, the paper flying from her hands to the edge of the stairs. Myrtle reached out to know her fate, her eyes burning, the smoke acrid and painful in her lungs. She dragged her body toward the staircase, her fingertips just touching the edge of the drawing, sending it fluttering down to become ashes below. She had no more strength. There just wasn't enough air.

The sound of breaking glass did not stir her. And when the man had climbed the stairs, he found her body limp.

A white sign in the yard, "Fire Sale," stood in contrast to the black streaked walls and charred lumber where the kitchen had been. A few people poked around as much to see the meager possessions as to find anything of value. Shaking their heads they murmured, "Poor woman," "It's a shame," and "This stuff won't even begin to pay all those bills."

    A young couple who'd been traveling through the area and weren't even neighbors came up. The woman said, "I'll give you seven dollars for this sketchbook. Maybe that'll help a little. I'm not much of an artist, myself, but—oh! There're already a couple of sketches in here. And I see some of the pages are torn out. Still, I'd like to help out. I'll still give you seven dollars for it. Who knows? It might inspire me."

The Picture

by Steve Workman

Her face stared at him across the years, sometimes disappearing for weeks or months at a time, but always returning to surprise and haunt him. She chased him in his dreams and, in his quietest moments, consoled his broken heart when life had been particularly cruel. Throughout high school, the wild years of college and beyond; from one girlfriend to the next; from one home to the next; though at times lost and then found and lost again; her image had survived so that whenever he searched in his wallet for that missing receipt, he would stumble across the black and white grade-school picture of his friend with the Mona Lisa smile.

Jeremy paid little attention to his obsession to always keep Madelyn's picture with him. He accepted it as a harmless, almost endearing, idiosyncrasy that was perhaps odd, but never disturbing . . . until today. He received a letter from Madelyn's mother who had somehow managed to track him down. Still living in the same small town in Indiana where Jeremy grew up, she said she needed to speak with him, in person, as soon as possible. But he could not imagine why. After all, it had been thirty-five years since he last saw her . . . at Madelyn's funeral . . . upon her death at the much-too-innocent age of twelve.

Jeremy lay in his bed that night trying to forget the remnants of a past he thought he buried a long time ago. Unfortunately for him, the letter was the last thing he saw as he reached over to turn out the light on his nightstand. The nightmares began almost before the room turned dark. He awoke in the middle of the night sweating and out of breath. Unable to fall back to sleep, he turned the light on and pulled the letter from the envelope to read once more . . .

> *Dear Jeremy,*
>
> *I know it's been a very long time. I can still remember the day of Madelyn's funeral as if it were yesterday, catching you in my arms when you fainted as you looked at her one last time. I know how close the two of you were. And who knows what may have been had she grown to become a woman.*
>
> *While I know the circumstances of her death were painful for you, to this very day, I tell anyone who asks that you did everything you could. Of course, few remember or ask about it anymore. But we will always remember, won't we Jeremy?*

Copyright © 2007 Steve Workman

After all these years, I recently met someone who seems to think that something else might have happened that day. As I have cancer and may have a limited amount of time before I meet my maker, I would appreciate you coming here as quickly as possible.

Sincerely,
Dorothy Perkins

Jeremy penned a note saying that he would try to swing by on a trip to Indianapolis in the next few weeks. As luck would have it, he was between jobs. He had been thinking about leaving the rat race of Los Angeles and returning to a part of America where neighbors did not erect walls or fences so they would not have to speak to one another; where an outstretched hand of friendship did not also leave the stench of being used afterwards. But then, it was never his choice to go to California after Madelyn died. That had been decided for him.

Upon arriving in Indianapolis, he rented a convertible and headed southwest in the direction of Crawfordsville, taking two-lane country roads most of the way. He put down the top and let his lungs savor the country air scrubbed clean by a thunderstorm the night before. Occasionally, when stopped at an intersection with no one behind him, he would shut off the engine so he could hear the katydids release their mating songs to drift on the sultry afternoon breeze. Images of he and Madelyn walking along the gravel road on the way home from school; the birthday parties; helping one another learn to ride a bicycle; pushing one another on the knotted rope swing and dropping into the river; these and a hundred other long-forgotten scenes began to replay themselves as he got closer to the place that he used to call home.

Near the edge of town, he turned into the main cemetery, and drove slowly past two large entry gates that hung precariously from a set of massive stone pillars. Nearly ten feet tall at either end, the gates had mostly rusted through their original coat of gold leaf paint. In the center of each gate was a large brass plate imprinted with the Angel Gabriel. The relief was now barely visible against years of neglect. The gates he remembered as a youth were far more impressive than these, especially late in the day, when the sun lay low on the horizon and a beam of light would shoot forth, as though the sun were the mirror and these gates marked the entrance to heaven itself.

He felt his throat tighten as he drove slowly along the one lane asphalt road until he came to the statue of the crying angel. Madelyn's grave would be nearby. Stepping out of the car, he surveyed the peaceful scene before him. Tiny American flags left over from July Fourth fluttered in a light breeze that made its way across the well-manicured lawn. He took a deep breath and savored the fragrance of freshly cut grass and the faded memory of helping his father mow the lawn on a hot summer afternoon.

Finally he came to the headstone he was looking for:

> Madelyn Perkins
> Beloved Daughter of Dorothy and Dan Perkins
> May 8, 1960-June 5, 1972

He pulled the picture of Madelyn from his wallet and gently caressed her faded image. Closing his eyes for a moment, he winced as images of the day she died began to breach the ramparts he had built to hold them back. The fact that they found her naked at the edge of the river while he admitted being with her, was all they needed to suspect. And the fact that his memory was less than clear about the events that transpired that day was all the prosecutor needed to convene a grand jury. The coroner pronounced her death as drowning precipitated by a blow to the back of her head. While the matter was not pursued in criminal court, it had not gone unnoticed by some local skeptics that Jeremy's father was also a former town mayor, a prominent lawyer in the local farming community, and a gracious host to the local barbecue scene. And while the evidence was not enough to bring him to trial, it was enough to find Jeremy guilty in the court of public opinion. Whether it was for his benefit or theirs, his parents excommunicated him to live with distant relatives in California.

As time passed and life moved on, most people forgot about what happened that day, except in the idle gaps of quiet dinner conversation when reminiscing about the good old days. No one remembers seeing Jeremy following Madelyn's death, although for years afterward, teenagers who parked by the river late at night would sometimes report seeing the silhouette of someone at the top of the hill overlooking the spot where Madelyn had died.

He kissed the single red rose that he had brought with him and placed it in the empty flower vase attached to Madelyn's headstone. Wrapped around the stem was a note that he had written before the he left Los Angeles.

With a full head of salt and pepper hair, an imposing 6 foot 3 inch frame, brooding eyebrows and square-cut jaw, Jeremy cut a memorable profile that made it difficult to be inconspicuous. To avoid the possibility of being recognized, he used side streets to get to the other side of town where Madelyn's mother lived. He found it remarkable that she was still living in the same house after all these years, but then life moved much slower, and sometimes not at all, in this part of the country. Surrounded by a fortress of maple and sycamore trees on three sides and the slow-moving waters of the Wabash River on the other, it had mostly withstood the seeds of progress to retain its Midwestern soul. The little market where he used to buy the latest pack of bubblegum baseball cards was still in business, albeit under a different name. An oncoming pickup truck waited while someone took a picture of a friend standing on the opposite side of the street. Even the blue eyes of strangers like Jeremy were met with a polite smile instead of the callous air of disinterest he had become accustomed to.

Turning onto the street where Mrs. Perkins lived brought a hint of a smile to his face. The maple trees in front of her single-story red brick house were much taller and the sidewalk was cracked from the roots that pushed up beneath it, but little else was changed . . . except for a For Sale sign in the front yard.

Jeremy took a deep breath and rang the doorbell. Thirty-five years. He could not imagine what she looked like. He rang the bell several times before finally opening the screen door and knocking loudly. A woman emerged from the house next door and walked to the edge of her front porch. "Can I help you?" she said, shielding her eyes from the late afternoon sun.

"I was looking for Mrs. Perkins. Do you know when she'll be back?"

The woman hesitated before answering. "I'm sorry . . . but she died some time ago."

Jeremy stared for a moment in disbelief. He quickly closed the screen door and walked down the steps to hear her better. "I'm sorry. Did you say . . . she died?"

"Yes. She passed away about six months ago," said the woman stepping closer to get a better look at him. "The house has been for sale ever since. Are you related?"

Jeremy took the envelope out of his pocket and carefully checked the postmark. "How could that be?" he said, rubbing his head in obvious confusion. "She just sent me this letter." Jeremy held the letter in the air.

The woman put one hand to her mouth, slowly stepped back into the shadows of her porch, and then, inextricably, stood in the doorway holding it open for him to come inside.

He stood frozen to the sidewalk in the heat of the afternoon as a chill swept through him. Slowly he began to realize what might be happening.

Jeremy noticed something uncomfortably familiar about the woman as he walked past her. She was pleasant looking with hazel eyes, although years of smoking had taken their toll on her delicate features. Her face was framed by waves of brunette hair that cascaded onto bare freckled shoulders, all framed by a white linen dress draped loosely over a full-figured body. Their eyes locked onto each other as he walked past her without speaking.

Her living room was decorated "messy comfortable." In the back of the room was a large bay window with a view of the river while, off to one side, was an easel with a half-finished oil-painting. Art supplies were left scattered across the coffee table. He stood awkwardly in the middle of the room.

"I'm Samantha. I was a friend of Mrs. Perkins." She did not offer to shake his hand.

"I'm Jeremy. But then I guess you knew that already."

"Can I get you something to drink? Lemonade or? . . ."

"That would be fine." While she disappeared into the kitchen, he walked over to the bay window and stared at a river that now boiled like a muddy stew from the recent rains. His stomach churned as he realized the spot where Madelyn died was around a bend just out of view.

The rattling of ice preceded her entrance into the living room. She set the tray on the coffee table and stood next to him watching the river tumble violently in the distance.

"Hauntingly beautiful, isn't it? After all these years, I keep thinking I'll paint something different. And yet every time, I get lost in another canvas that starts to look like the one I just finished." She nodded toward a wall that was covered with oil paintings of the river at different times of the season.

"I think you should know that I didn't write the letter," she finally added. "Mrs. Perkins did. She wrote it right before she died but I didn't mail it until a few weeks ago."

He looked at her, incredulous that she would hold onto a letter containing the last wishes of a dying woman. "I presume you know what it was that she wanted to say to me."

She sat down and looked nervously out the window. "I know coming back here must have been difficult for you, but I'm glad you did. I think you'll want to hear what I have to say. Please sit down."

Jeremy's heart began pounding.

"I know the story you told about the day Madelyn died . . . but I also know something else happened that day that needs to be told."

Jeremy's face turned red as he stood up and bolted angrily for the door. "After all these years, people are still second guessing what happened. I should have known better than to come back here."

"Why did you, then? Was everyone supposed to welcome you back like a war hero?" said Samantha, standing to confront him.

Jeremy's hand rested on the doorknob as he contemplated an answer. "To give some peace to a dying woman . . . and perhaps myself in the process."

"Then come with me," she begged him. "I want to show you something."

Jeremy hesitated. He knew coming back was going to be painful in ways that he could not even imagine, but then he was tired of running from the nightmares that periodically leaped out of the dark and tried to smother him. He turned to face her. "What was it you wanted to show me?"

Samantha led him out the back door where they walked to the river's edge. With no fences separating her neighbors on either side, it was easy to access a narrow trail that paralleled the river. They shared small talk most of the way. He learned that Samantha bought the house next to Mrs. Perkins a few years ago after living most of her life on the opposite side of the river. She was home schooled, which explains why Jeremy did not remember her growing up. And she had spent much of her time indoors after taking up painting at an early age. But there was also an interesting twist to her passion: all of her paintings were of the same scene.

He followed in her footsteps and they followed the trail to the top of a hill with a large rain tree that spread its vast canopy over the entire summit. Its size was almost mythical, and it was accepted local lore that anyone who stood under it when dropping its yellow blossoms would find true love.

Upon reaching the edge of the clearing, he abruptly stopped. "Please tell me where we're going and why?" he pleaded.

She turned slowly to look at him and smiled. "We're here." She walked to the base of the rain tree, pulled back the underbrush and motioned for him to come closer. Carved into the trunk of the tree was a short poem along with the author's initials.

Jeremy's eyes began to water. "I carved those words after Madelyn died, but it looks like I did this yesterday."

"I know," sighed Samantha. "I come here every now and then . . . and re-carve them. I used to come up here late at night when the moon was full and no one else was around, but then rumors started flying that you, or your ghost, had been spotted." She looked at him. "I stopped coming after that, not because of the rumors, but because there were times when I felt you were standing next to me. In any case, I don't have to recarve the words anymore. The tree is mature enough that I think they will always be there." She sat down on a bench nearby and looked at the ground as she spoke. "Tell me again what you remember about that day."

Jeremy didn't answer immediately. He walked to the edge of the clearing and watched the roiling waters below them. The wind rustled through the trees trying to stay ahead of another storm front that was building in the distance. The blackness beneath it was in stark contrast to the warm sunlit spot where they now stood. For some reason, he found it easy to be vulnerable in her presence. He stared into the distance as an all too familiar scene unfolded once more in his mind.

"Madelyn and I used to sit on this hill," he began. "We used to talk for hours on end about school, homework, who liked who, the weather, what we were going to do with the rest of our lives . . ." He grew silent as if he could still hear the echoes of those conversations.

"It was very different that summer," he continued. "It was hot and dry. We hadn't had any rain for weeks. We had to make sure we walked on the upwind side of the road so we wouldn't choke on the clouds of dust kicked up by a passing car. It was also the last day of school. Everyone was excited about the long summer ahead. Madelyn and I got off the bus and started walking home, but then decided to go down to the river and jump in to cool off."

Jeremy smiled. "As we got near the river, Madelyn dropped everything and started running toward the rope swing. She jumped and swung out over the river laughing. I remember the mischievous look on her face as she looked back at me and then let go, dropping into the river, clothes and all. She swam back to shore, grabbed the extra rope that we kept nearby and tied it around my chest. I didn't know how to swim so, this way, she could pull me back to shore."

"You must have trusted her very much," she interrupted.

Jeremy shifted his gaze and looked directly at her. "I trusted her with my life."

"It was the second time when it happened," he said in a more serious tone. "The water level was so low we could see some rocks just a few feet from shore so we were dropping out past them . . . where it was deeper. Madelyn lost her grip and fell backwards, hitting her head on some rocks just below the surface. She rolled over face down and started drifting down the river toward the opposite bank. I ran over the railroad trestle to get to the other side and jumped in to get her. It didn't matter that I couldn't swim. I reached out and . . . I could feel my fingers touching hers, when . . . the rope snapped against my chest. Someone was pulling me back to shore. When I felt my feet touching bottom, I stood up and tried to open my eyes to see who was pulling me back in. But I was choking and my eyes were full of water. All I could see was the back of someone as they ran away through the trees. They never believed me when I told them that someone else was there that day."

There was a long pause as they looked into each others' eyes.

"I was playing near the river that afternoon," she finally began. "It wasn't the first time that I noticed the two of you sitting up here. For some reason, I felt a connection with you from a distance over the years. I was watching you through the trees that day. You left out the part where the two of you decided to take your clothes off and go skinny dipping. For someone who was only nine years old and who had spent the better part of every Sunday being lectured about temptation and the fires of hell . . . " she smiled. "Well, I guess I wanted to jump in the river and join you."

"You didn't see me when you ran across the trestle to the other side of the river and jumped into the water. I was terrified when I realized what was happening. When you started to struggle, I saw the end of the rope lying near shore, so I ran down and pulled you back in. Remember, I was only nine. So I ran away . . . at first."

Jeremy looked surprised. "What do you mean 'at first'? I never saw you again. You never came forward."

"I was halfway home when, for some reason, I stopped and ran back. When I got there, I looked down and saw that you had managed to reach Madelyn." Samantha's voice started to crack as she spoke. "You were cradling her in your arms . . . and crying."

Jeremy looked away. He was more comfortable crying late at night when he was all alone.

Samantha continued. "You started pounding on her chest. Harder and harder. If she wasn't already dead, I thought you were going to kill her. And then . . . you stopped. I watched as you leaned over her and kissed her on the lips and said goodbye. You ran back to the other side, put on your clothes and ran to get help." She looked at him anxiously. "And that's when it happened."

"When what happened?" he asked.

"When she threw up!" Samantha waited for the revelation to sink in. "Jeremy, she was still alive!"

He looked at her in disbelief. "But, Madelyn was dead when we got back."

"That's why we're here," Samantha answered. "It's why I asked Mrs. Perkins to write the letter and why I waited until after she died to mail it. It's why I take sleeping pills every night secretly hoping I'll never wake up in the morning." Samantha pulled back the sleeve of her blouse and held out her right arm.

Jeremy gingerly held her wrist in the open palm of his hand, careful not to touch the scars that were still prominent from the self-mutilation. She paused to let him grasp the enormity of her own grief.

"When she threw up," she continued, "she was on her back. She must have started to drown all over again."

"What did you do?"

Samantha placed her hand over her mouth as she started to shake. "Nothing. I did nothing."

"But you ran down to the shore and pulled me back in. Why wouldn't you help Madelyn?"

"I have asked myself that question for the last thirty-five years," said Samantha. She looked at him hoping he would understand. "Perhaps . . . I somehow hoped she would . . . go away. Perhaps I wanted to be her. Perhaps I wanted to be the one who sat up here on this hill and talked to you every day. I tried to forget what happened, but never could. It was only after years of therapy, that my mother happened to say something to me in a moment of anger that was the first clue to why I might have felt the way I did. She said I was adopted when I was two years old. She tried to apologize for making the comment at the time and said it wasn't true, but I knew it was. I could never find any information about my biological parents . . . until I told Mrs. Perkins about what happened the day Madelyn died."

"You told Mrs. Perkins?"

"I suppose I was subconsciously reaching out to her when I bought the house next to her. When I heard she was going into the hospital, I decided I needed her to know what happened that day before it was too late. There were so many rumors that circulated after they found Madelyn with no clothes on. I was so frightened when I told her. She just brushed the back of her hand against my cheek and thanked me. She said she knew I must have suffered like her over the years. And she thought I should tell you as well. While she grieved about Madelyn's death for a long time afterward, I think she always loved you like a son. And then she decided to return the favor by telling me something else . . . that she knew that I had been adopted and who my biological parents were. Jeremy . . . I'm your sister!"

Jeremy stood transfixed without any expression on his face. It belied the storm raging within him as he struggled with the idea that Madelyn might have lived that day had he stayed with her. And yet this is why he had come back . . . to reconnect. After being ripped from his family and his life destroyed, he had found a remnant of that family.

The emotional torment inside him finally gave way, as he reached out and cradled her face between his hands and kissed her on the forehead. They hugged each other for a long time afterward as the rain began pouring down upon them.

Every two weeks, the caretaker of the local cemetery removed the dead flowers, letters and other debris left behind by loved ones. In the course of doing so, he occasionally took the time to read some of them and forwarded the more poignant ones to a writer at the local newspaper. Upon removing the wilted rose from the vase on Madelyn's grave, he noticed the letter attached to its stem. He could not have known that the same words were carved years ago into the trunk of tree at the top of a hill nearby:

> I leave my heart
> For you to hold
> To keep you warm
> When it's too cold
> I leave my life
> I have no more
> That you might use it
> Like once before
>
> J+M

Robert Bly Changed My Life
by Pat Coyle

"Out beyond ideas of wrongdoing and rightdoing, there is a field. I will meet you there." Rumi (Persian Poet and Mystic, 1207-1273)

It is January 2007. KQED, our local NPR station, announced a program at Stanford—Rumi: an 800th Birthday Celebration with Robert Bly. I love Rumi, but I really wanted to hear Robert Bly.

Robert Bly changed my life.

In April 1969, I went to a poetry reading against the Vietnam War in Boulder, Colorado. Robert Bly was there, along with Lawrence Ferlinghetti, Gary Snyder, Allen Ginsberg, and Robert Creeley.

I was twenty-one, due to graduate from Colorado School of Mines in May. I'd been accepted for graduate school in mathematics at Berkeley, Purdue, and Tulane. I was opposed to the Vietnam War and the draft.

I first became aware of Vietnam as a high school sophomore, at debate and extemporaneous speech competitions. You would draw questions on current event topics, have thirty minutes to prepare an answer to the question, and then speak on the topic for seven minutes. At one competition, I spoke of the thousands of United States military advisors we had in South Vietnam and of the domino theory—if one land in a region came under the influence of Communists, then more would follow in a domino effect. It was just a current event topic to me then.

My opposition had grown over the years as I learned more about the history of Indochina, the role of the French, the War, and our deepening involvement there.

Images and a new vocabulary of horror streamed through our three TV networks' nightly news shows with unprecedented immediacy. Body counts. Americans scrambling out of helicopter doors. Bloodied wounded being moved on stretchers. Burning thatched huts. Bombs. High-speed machine-gun fire. Incendiary fragmentation grenades. Napalm. Agent orange ravaging the landscape and people below.

After a ferocious fight over a place called Ben Tre, an American Army major said he had been forced to destroy the village in order to save it.

On a city street, the Saigon police chief fired a bullet into the head of a Viet Cong dressed in civilian clothes. Associated Press photographer Eddie Adams captured the moment and won a Pulitzer for it. The photo editor who first looked at the film, said, "I saw . . . the perfect newspicture—the perfectly framed and exposed 'frozen moment' of an event which I felt instantly would become representative of the brutality of the Vietnam War."

Steven Boals, my high school friend two years ahead of me, had been killed in Vietnam. By 1969, our troop count had grown to 500,000. Over 36,000 Americans had died there. In the end, it would cost more than 58,000 American lives, 350,000 American casualties, and between one and two million Vietnamese deaths.

David Harris, the famous draft resister, had given over a thousand speeches saying the war was a crime against everything America was meant to be, and urging any man called to the draft to join him and refuse to go. He would soon be in Federal prison.

In addition to the draft's role in sending men to Vietnam, I had become opposed to the nature of the draft itself. I was also angry that Selective Service had eliminated draft deferments for graduate school.

The issues started years earlier. From when I was ten years old, the Space Race shaped my education and, later, my thoughts about career options. The Space Race started after the Soviet Union successfully launched Sputnik in 1957. In response, the United States launched a huge effort to regain technological supremacy. The National Defense Education Act, the most far-reaching federally-sponsored education initiative in the nation's history, authorized expenditures of more than one billion dollars for a wide range of reforms: new school construction, fellowships and loans to encourage promising students to seek higher education, new efforts in vocational education to meet critical manpower shortages in the defense industry, and a host of other programs.

I was a product of this national initiative and now I resented it.

I had become aware of, and fundamentally opposed to the draft's role in this initiative. Selective Service called it "channeling." The main purpose of the draft was not to deliver men into the Army, but to channel millions of registrants into pursuits deemed vital to the Nation's best interest. As Selective Service publication 899.125 put it, "One of the major products of the Selective Service classification process is the channeling of manpower into many endeavors, occupations, and activities that are in the national interest.. . . . Selective Service processes do not compel people by edict as in foreign systems to enter pursuits having to do with essentiality and progress. They go because they know that by going they will be deferred.. . . From the individual's viewpoint, he is standing in a room which has been made uncomfortably warm. Several doors are open, but they all lead to various forms of recognized patriotic service to the Nation.. . . ."

I hated this process of using the pressure of the draft and deferments to channel people into activities in the national interest.

That was my state of mind, when we went to the poetry reading against the Vietnam War in Boulder. To get there, John May and I drove north, from Golden to Boulder, on two-lane Highway 93—cruising along the edge of the foothills of the Rockies with the prairie rolling out to Denver and beyond.

When we got to the University of Colorado, Macky Auditorium was filling up fast. The crowd ran the gamut. There were older academics, solid middle-aged people from Boulder's progressive liberal community, longhaired guys and hippie-looking women with the smell of patchouli oil and pot trailing behind them. There were also button-down shirt, shorthaired guys like me.

The auditorium buzzed with an increasing atmosphere of anticipation and conversations as people filled the room, and we waited for the program to begin.

The poets came onto the stage to the enthusiastic applause of the crowd. They also ranged the spectrum of appearance. Snyder, longhaired but with a look of the Zen practitioner he was; Ginsburg, wild haired and bearded; Creeley, looking more traditional with his closely trimmed beard. Bly wore a serape with black markings on a light background.

The poets sat or stood on the stage in casual disarray. Some milled around while talking with each other and passing around a bottle of tequila. Then they read and continued to pass the bottle of tequila around.

When his time came, Bly read *The Teeth Mother Naked at Last*.

The crowd exploded with applause. I responded to Bly in my gut, in my heart, in my whole body. I was overwhelmed and powerfully moved by his imagery of the terrible choices our government had made, and the actions we were personally being asked to take.

I recently talked to John May, one of the three other Colorado School of Mines students who turned in their draft cards about the same time I did. I asked him about this poetry reading.

"Yes, I remember it, I was there with you," John said, "Ginsburg and Snyder were there and the others, too. Ginsburg read *Howl* and accompanied himself with a tiny squeezebox accordion—it was a little weird. There was also a Buddhist monk chanting. The whole poetry reading was incredible. I remember Bly reading. It was that Earth Mother poem of his. Bly's reading was absolutely incredible. You could see his whole body swaying and moving on the stage as his voice filled the room. You were drawing in a notebook, trying to sketch the energy as he read."

Hearing Robert Bly's poetry that night catalyzed a decision that changed my life. In his 1969 "Acceptance of the National Book Award for Poetry," Bly said that Americans want a life of feeling without a life of suffering.

I thought long and hard about it that night. I was ready to step forward even knowing I would suffer for it. On April 29, 1969, I wrote a letter to my draft board in Santa Fe, New Mexico. "Gentlemen: I am returning my registration and draft classification cards to you to indicate that I will no longer cooperate with the Selective Service System. My non-cooperation is based primarily on two factors: the Vietnam War and the nature of the draft itself."

I knew this would mean they would reclassify me 1-A and speed up my induction process. When they tried to induct me, I would refuse. This was a felony and carried a one to five year prison sentence and/or a ten thousand dollar fine. In Colorado, the average sentence was three years with no fine.

My mother's journal entries for May first and second, 1969 read "… we received a letter from Pat with a copy of the letter he wrote his draft board returning his cards. He wrote us, 'I am sorry that I have had to choose this route since I know it will cause me and you a lot of anguish—more pain for you, I am sure. The alternatives were more painful for me' . . . I knew it would happen. I've listened to him for a year and a half. Maybe he hoped it wouldn't be necessary. I did. I just kept hoping."

(familiarity)
by Ian Ray Armknecht

last chance on the spinning wheel—
no more subtle daisies for the
omnivores with their facsimiles
and their treasure maps.
taste the winter-white ice and
breathe in and out every colour.
tomorrow our day comes on the heads
of delicate harbingers
and leaves in our mouths the empty
taste of ash and autumn.

My Rightful Father
by Grace Ryan

You squint over the steering wheel at an incautious intersection
And even the poems stop.
My mind sighs
With a yearning for memories that I long forgot I never had.
There's a sense of me tap dancing on top of myself
As if I deserve your attention
As if silence would slice the umbilical cord
And I would be lost inside you
Swimming alone in seas that are my own.
I forget
Sometimes
That word—
The one you've never said
Because you want me
free.

Fatherhood
by Tom Darter

    I just read some poems
        about fatherhood,
    and I realized—
        no one ever told me
        it was supposed to be
            amazing,
                life-changing,
        an epiphany.

    I just thought (I think) that
    it was one of those things
        that one does:
    Eat, sleep, grow up, go to school,
        fall in love, get married,
        try to do some good.
    Have children.

    So I wasn't prepared
        for the awe of it all:
    Didn't know about the awe
        I was supposed to feel.
    And so I don't remember acting (or reacting)
        with reverence, awe, and amazement—
            all those feelings I
            should have had.

Still, I see pictures
    of me with my children,
    and I realize that
I was so in the moment
    of playing on the beach with that one,
    of gazing at the new face of that one,
    of holding the sleeping new body of that one,
that there was no "me" left over to save the memory.

And yes, I am blessed.
How else to explain
    these three amazing beings
    that I am so proud
    to call my children.

My Daughter's Wedding
by Charan Sue Wollard

I expected my sister would rush in
bearing luggage, gifts, her entire entourage,
excuses wadded like old paper in her hand,
to stand beside me on the shore of Lake Tahoe
where orange sunlight sparkled on turquoise water
the only clear, dry day that October

The bride radiated like a new star
ecru gown, lace veil, a shock of red roses in her arms
Before her, a procession of her sisters and their daughters
her beaming father walked her down the aisle
feet crushing fragrant petals on the white carpet

I waited in the front row
a second cousin on my father's side stood behind me
"Where are the others?" she whispered
Later the DJ played "Celebration"
we danced until midnight.

Amber Afternoons

by Tania Selden

The meaning of the word "afternoon" is many layers deep for me, due to sounds, sights, and touches I experienced over several months when I was five.

My parents lived in an early twentieth century wooden house in Oakland that had an elegant three-part bay window in the master bedroom. To subdue the rich, southwestern light, they installed three ivory-colored cloth shades you could pull down to cover the windows. When the afternoon sun filtered through these shades, the whole bedroom filled with rich, dim, amber light, so that it resembled a Veronese painting.

During my first year of public school, I had to take afternoon naps. I did not object, as far as I remember, to what became a ritual. After arriving home from kindergarten, I would greet my mother, put down my belongings and follow her into the master bedroom. She would peel back the pale green, lightweight rayon Jacquard coverlet, the wool blankets, the white sheets. I would take off my good school clothes and snuggle under the cool sheets, my head on one of the feather pillows. Mother went to the tall windows, reached up high, and pulled down each shade by the string-covered ring that dangled from its center. If the sunlight outside was strong and unclouded, the light in the bedroom metamorphosed to dim amber from bright clear. I slept easily in such a quiet, safe realm.

But the sensory picture included something else. After a few days of after-school quiet time, I realized that I could count on a regularly occurring, lazy sound which became part of my amber afternoon ambiance: the drone of an airplane. The single engine plane flew near my house and over Park Boulevard the same time every day, at the same elevation. I have often wondered what its true mission was, even though at the time I accepted the sound of it as part of my tapestry of rest. Even now, when I am aware of the drone of a small plane nearby, I can re-enter the protected, golden space of quiet afternoons in my parents' bedroom.

Sunday
by Jennifer Lock

Under fingers wrinkled
filled with ages of dirt

Tenuous brown pants
soiled caked cuffs
knees and ass worn
shoes filled with pebbles

Unshaven face
sun dried thirsty lips
pleading for moisture

Exasperation stalking his
tired body
Fighting a private battle

He digs to choke a weed
from its deep root
another will grow

A congregation passes kicking up dust
excited noise as the Sunday service begins

His eyes burn through them
revealing mist-filled memories

Years drop and hours are numbers
elaborately viewed

Mourning with music
a verse from Psalms delivered

Grave eyes unleash tears
at last the final verse

and all he has is her garden.

My Parents' Bedroom

by Tania Selden

A handsome bay window with window seats dominated my parents' bedroom. It was the first thing you saw when you peeked in. The next obvious thing was the dark walnut double bed with its carved oak panel on the headboard. The bed matched Daddy's highboy. He had a desk right by the entry door; it was dark oak and had cubby holes inside. If you pulled down the front, you could use that surface for writing. Mother's dark oak dresser was the curvy piece in the room. Silver-framed pictures of Grandma and Grandpa sat on it. Two side chairs with caned seats and backs, and two bedside stands completed the furniture. They had just enough to fit the room.

Every Sunday morning before church my parents read *The Oakland Tribune* in bed. They looked cozy underneath their white sheets, propped up with puffy feather pillows, and covered with wool blankets, and a light green rayon Jacquard weave coverlet with scalloped edges. Daddy was especially keen on "the funnies," following them all. He read the front page right after the cartoons.

On one memorable Sunday morning when I was five and a half, my father and mother called me to their bedroom extra early. Daddy held the first section of the paper, turned to the front page, between his hands. I could see that the headlines were huge, taking up half of the front page. Tall, black, fat letters shouted that Japan had attacked the United States' fleet of ships in Pearl Harbor in Hawaii in a surprise early morning coup, and my father did his best to explain it to his five-year-old child. I understood instantly, but not the facts. My father's serious face and deep, even voice conveyed his fear and horror, which became mine. Now, on my daily walks to and from kindergarten, I checked the sky for falling bombs. I feared the searchlights slicing the night sky, hated the eerie air raid sirens that meant we had to put up our blackout curtains, and caught mother's fear whenever Daddy was sent away from Oakland to Nevada to put up telephone wires.

My parents' bedroom, where for the previous three months I had been experiencing restorative afternoon naps in safety, comfort, and peace, had become the setting for my childhood introduction to war.

A Peach Cobbler Tale

by Karen L. Hogan

My grandmother was born into a very precarious world.
Women died in childbirth.
Men died in farm accidents.
The Spanish Flu Pandemic of 1918 took people indiscriminately.
"They dropped like flies," my grandmother would say. "They'd get it—and the next day they were gone. It was just awful."

By the time I joined the world, miracle drugs and vaccines seemed to make the world a less precarious place.

She was grateful for our safety, but precarious was a familiar world to her. She and her sister, my great aunt Bird, played dueling storytelling to keep that world alive. So when I came to the table that day in my thirteenth year, the red, pustule-protruding zit on my nose slathered in Clearasil, they were ready with stories of a tragic nature.

"Why, I knew a man who squeezed a blackhead on his nose one night." Grandma plopped the spoonful of mashed potatoes onto her plate. "He woke up sicker than a dog the next morning. Three days later—he woke up dead." She held the bowl of potatoes in midair. "See there's these things that lead right up to your brain from your nose. If you squeeze a pimple on your nose, you could squeeze the infection right back up into your brain!"

"They call the nose the triangle of death."

She passed the bowl of potatoes to Great Aunt Bird, who picked up the gauntlet without blinking an eye. "Well, you know that gal—I recollect her name was Naomi. You know she went with Isaac there for a while—before Isaac started dating me. I think she started seeing Jacob right after we was married." She plunged the spoon into the mashed potatoes.

"Well, she and Jacob was gonna get married themselves. She had the dress she made and they was planning on moving out to old man Smith's place out there in the country. I was gonna bring my peach cobbler for the reception. You know I had picked those big juicy peaches from the tree we had in the front yard there." Great Aunt Bird slapped the potatoes onto her plate and passed them to my brother.

"And then three days before the wedding, she had that little speck on her nose and she fiddled with it. And Lordy, she just got so sick." Aunt Bird sipped her iced tea, wiped the bottom of the glass with her napkin, dabbed at her lips, leaned back, and delivered the news about Naomi like it was the curve ball that would strike out the home-run king. "She died on her wedding day. And I made that peach cobbler for her funeral instead of her wedding."

Great Aunt Bird sliced off a hunk of butter, dropped it onto her potatoes, and passed the butter dish to my grandmother, who picked it up and, without skipping a beat, began another tale of someone lost to the triangle of death. They continued their dueling stories of tragic deaths by blackheads and pimples as we made our way through the meatloaf, mashed potatoes, corn, and green beans.

As I cleared the table, Grandmother brought out her peach cobbler, and with it, her big guns—the "Millie" story.

"Why, poor ol' Millie. She wasn't but about twenty-two year old. She had just had her third baby not a week before. You remember, Birdie, it was the year of that snow storm that liked to killed us all." She turned to my father, "Now don't you be shy—you take as much of that cobbler as you want."

The purse strings around Great Aunt Bird's mouth were starting to pucker.

"Now, Millie and her family had just finished dinner. She had made a real good roast chicken and a berry pie for dessert. She put the kids to bed and then saw that boil on her nose and thought, well, maybe I'll just get rid of it.

"So she squeezed and squeezed, and she got rid of it, all right. And then she went to bed. We saw her at church the next day. You remember, don't you, Birdie?" She passed her peach cobbler to Great Aunt Bird.

"I thought," my grandmother continued, "that Millie looked just a little peak-id. So I asked her, 'Why, Millie, how do you feel?'

"And she said, 'Well, I feel just a bit peak-id, you know. The new baby and all.'

"None of us thought anything about it, but then the next morning, we found out that she just didn't wake up. And she left those three little kids for Ben to take care of all by hisself."

Great Aunt Birdie's pressed lips were tighter than dried egg whites. Tragic death of young new mother—of three, no less—trumped bride-died-on-her wedding day anytime.

Grandma always sort of had the advantage. She was the older of the two. And while everyone complimented my great aunt Bird on her peach cobbler—they always asked my grandmother for her recipe.

I, meanwhile, was quietly freaking out. All through dinner I thought back to the blackheads and pimples I had squeezed. Was one of them stuck behind my forehead, waiting for the right moment to strike my brain? I hadn't known about the triangle of death.

But then, neither had Millie.

I had waited all day for the zit to ripen. The last sock hop of the year was the next day and Nancy had talked to Will and it turned out he wasn't mad at me for striking him out at the noon-time baseball game after all and he was gonna ask me to dance—finally.

It was my turn to wash dishes. As I swabbed repeatedly at a glass I began to imagine the look on Will's face when he confronted Mt. Zit.

My brother, who was drying dishes, smelled blood and moved in for the kill. "So I hear Santa's got an opening."

I glanced at him sideways so I wouldn't have to see the red bulb on the end of my nose. "What do you mean?"

"Oh, nothin'." He began humming "Rudolph the Red Nosed Reindeer."

My brother was an expert at submarine warfare, his periscope always riding the surface, looking for ways to humiliate me—especially when it came to my pimples. He would pound on the bathroom door and scream at me that if I would stop picking my pimples he could get into the bathroom sooner. His timing was impeccable. He always caught me in mid-squeeze.

I tried to ignore his humming through the glasses, the dishes, the pots, and, finally, the peach cobbler pan.

My bedroom was right across from the bathroom. My brother was coming out of his bedroom, heading for the bathroom, so I leapt across the hallway and slammed the door just as he started sprinting. I stared into the mirror and thought about Will.

Was he worth waking up dead for?

My grandmother's words came back to me: you *could* squeeze the infection back up into your brain.

Could.

I had an out. I decided to seal off the passageways. Very carefully, I placed two fingers, one on top and one on the bottom of the zit, and gently nudged its contents up and away from where I imagined the opening to the passageway that led to my brain would be. Then very quickly I pulled my hands away from my face.

I stared at the mirror. Nothing happened.

I placed fingers on either side of the zit, and again nudged its contents up and away from the opening to the pathway that led to my brain.

I stared at the mirror. Nothing happened.

With the opening sealed off, I got serious about conquering the zit. I squeezed. Top to bottom. Side to side. Top to bottom. Side to side. Top to bottom. Side to side. Until finally with a soft "patooi," followed by a light "thpft," the zit shot off my nose and landed on the mirror.

Bam! Bam! Bam!

"What are you doin' in there—defyin' the triangle of death?"

"Shut up! If you must know, I'm taping my spit curls to my face."

I poured Bonney Doon 1006 lotion on my nose. I figured that Bonney Doon would get sucked up any passageway I hadn't sealed off and mow down rogue germs on their way to my brain.

I tore off a piece of clear tape, and placed it over the carefully styled spit curl on my right cheek. I tore off another, and pasted the spit curl on my left cheek.

Bam! Bam! Bam!

I was starting to enjoy his impatience.

I taped my bangs to my forehead, then admired my handiwork in the mirror. I thought about leaving the zit on the mirror, just for spite, but cleaned it off.

"About time, Rudolph!" my brother said. I kept my head down so he couldn't see the details of my nose.

I climbed into bed, pulled the cool sheets up around me. Lesley Gore was singing "Its My Party and I'll Cry If I Want To" on my clock radio.

My nose felt funny. I began to imagine that an army of bacteria had broken through the sealed passageway and were streaming up either side of my nose, ready to ram the barricade to my brain.

I started wondering what it would feel like to wake up dead. Would my brother be sorry, or happy? Would he sing "Rudolph the Red Nosed Reindeer" at my funeral?

I thought, maybe if I just don't go to sleep, I can't wake up dead. But if I didn't sleep, what would I look like the next day? What if I fell asleep at the sock hop? All the while, the bacteria were streaming up either side of my nose.

Lesley Gore was singing "Now, It's Judy's Turn to Cry" on my clock radio. My brother farted in the next room. Sun streamed through my window.

I woke up—alive!

My brother was coming out of his bedroom just as I reached the bathroom and slammed the door. I slowly pulled the tape off my spit curls and bangs. The zit had faded to a light pink —light enough for Clearasil to cover it completely.

Bam! Bam! Bam!

"What's taking you so long? Picking your pimples again?

Finally, my brother's timing was off. I took my time teasing my hair and left a cloud of Aqua Net for him to walk into.

Will didn't show up at the sock hop. Something about an appointment at the dermatologist, Nancy heard. I never did get to dance with him. My dad got a new job that summer and we moved away before school started.

My great aunt Bird and grandmother continued to savor the precariousness of life— and to compete. On my grandmother's ninetieth birthday, she danced and flirted with the musician while he sang "You Are my Sunshine." Great Aunt Bird seized the opportunity. She snuck up behind Grandma and whispered in her ear, "What would Dad think of you dancin' and carryin' on this way?"

Great Aunt Bird had a heart attack and died about a month later, before they had a chance to duel again. So Great Aunt Bird won on a technicality.

I was with my Grandmother when she drew her last breath. It was about two months after her ninety-ninth birthday. She'd been active, spry, and alert up until that morning. When she fainted, we took her to the hospital where the doctor told us she was in heart failure. There was nothing anyone could do.

She was clearly in discomfort. I asked her if she was afraid.

"Oh, no," she said. "Dyin' would be easier than this. I wish the Lord would take me home."

Five minutes later she was gone.

My grandmother was right. Life is precarious.
I never got around to getting her peach cobbler recipe.

Government Cheerios
by Jennifer Lock

I wanted breakfast this morning.
The milk thick stench
clusters slump to the bowl

Another night long into weeks
of shots and cigarettes

No spoons are ever clean

"Honey, bring Momma a beer!"

That feeling of reality stung my senses
as I felt another mistake taking shape

The sun sharp rays piercing my eyes
How easy it could be to laze about in the light
for the pure pleasure of pain

A stranger to me, this tan lady
lying in her lawn chair
smoking a cigarette and drinking

Her skin looks like a fake leather jacket
gravel voice echoes
old belly wrinkles over
with pitted pockets of cellulite

She tries to seduce a young man
he smiles, quite embarrassed for himself
tainted by this woman falling drunk
'by noon on Tuesday'

The sun reflected in the drops of sweat
running off her mustache

Drip
I can see my reflection for a moment
thin and pathetic
I intended to ask for our food stamps
before she passed out.

Before Smog
by Kathy Mima

In my yard
was the scent of orange blossoms,
the green green grass except
where the pool stood and our dog made muddy tracks
playing chase with us.

In my yard
I drew the magic
wand and colors grew,
flew, rising and swir-
ling all around.

In my yard
it was a sunny morning, a sunny afternoon,
the blue California sky fresh
with sea air
(that was before they invented smog).

In my yard
I left my jelly sandwich
and grasped my magic wand
with sticky fingers as the Bubble Joy
label was beginning to melt off.

In my yard
as I danced and sang to the bugs,
I promised that I would always love
bubbles.

In my yard
was the scent of orange blossoms.

Thunderheads

by Ethel Mays

Mountains peer over the shoulders of sunburned hills, jealously glaring down on fields and pastures made green by waters once owned by pack ice and snow. Only the highest peaks still boast white, unsullied mantles. All else is scorched granite, laid to waste by deadly summer sun. Thunderheads pound on a wide open sky.

Mick's wrangling with a posthole digger when I ride up. His shirt's off and I see all his back and arm muscles. He's very tall and what my mama calls rangy. My face gets hot, but that goes away before he looks up.

"Hey, girl," he says. "What're you doin' out here?" He smiles and I can't hide my face in time.

"Brought ya' some lunch. Hungry?" I jump down from my horse's bare back, putting it between him and me. My face feels like it's on fire. The rucksack I have slung over my shoulder slides behind me and bumps my backside.

"Sure, now that you mention it," Mick says, "I could eat. I was just 'bout ready to rest a spell."

Mick's pickup is parked under a tree close by and I head over to it, leading my horse on loose reins. Mick leaves his digging, slings on his shirt, and joins me in the shade. He takes my horse's reins from me and pats him on the neck. Then he asks me, "So. When'd you get nerve enough to get up on Ricochet?"

"I've ridden him lots," I say. "'Sides, he was the only one available today."

Before I put Ricochet's bridle on him today, I made sure I had a halter on him first and a lead rope on that so I could tie him up proper later. Mick takes off the bridle and hands it to me. He looks at me real serious for a minute, then gives me a little nod. He unlooses the lead rope I have looped around Ricochet's neck and ties it to a branch so my horse can reach some grass but not trip himself. "Well, ya' handled him good enough to get 'im here. I s'pose you best get 'im back the same way." Ricochet starts cropping grass like a greedy pig. He's too busy to pay us any mind.

"Hope so," I say and give him a sassy grin. "Here, you hold this a minute." I hand him back the bridle and dive into my bag. I pull out a tablecloth and set the bag down so I can spread the cloth out on the grass. Then I take out sandwiches wrapped in wax paper and a bottle of cold lemonade I packed. I put all of this in the middle of the table cloth and flop down on one side of it all. I'm through talking about a horse I have no business on. I'm eleven-and-a-half, almost grown, and have a man to feed. No horse is going to get in the way of that.

Mick lays the bridle on the edge of the table cloth and takes off his beat-up cowboy hat. He has hair that I think is black like a raven's. He tosses his hat on a corner of the tablecloth and sits down on the other side of the picnic.

"So what do we have here?" he says, unwrapping one of the sandwiches.

"Just ham and cheese," I say.

"You make 'em yourself?"

I nod. "This morning. Mama cooked the ham last night."

Mick smiles. "Then these here sandwiches are food fit for kings an' queens an' all things royal an' elegant."

I wrinkle my nose at him and giggle. Sometimes he mixes in fairy tale talk. But I still like it, even though I'm almost grown.

We eat the sandwiches and pass the lemonade between us. It's hot and dry today, but there's a little breeze and it's cool under the tree. Mick's been working on getting posts into the ground for new fences on the Edwards' property. I've ridden out about five miles to see him today.

Part way through our lunch, Mick cocks his head to one side and catches me with his cool look. "Your mama know you're out here?"

I shake my head slowly. "Not exactly."

"Um-hm."

I squirm a little bit.

"She know you out ridin'?"

"Yeah . . ." I duck my head and look at the flower pattern on the tablecloth.

"Next time, you tell her where you're goin', okay?"

I don't want to, but I nod. Mick's seven years older than me so I have to.

"How're ya' gettin' home once you get Ricochet put away proper?" he asks.

"Walk, I s'pose. Maybe call up from Bonnie's."

Mick's face and voice get soft. "You hang out with Bonnie. I'll come get ya an' run ya home when I get done out here."

I light up. "Stay for dinner if Mama says okay?"

He smiles. "We'll see."

I know the chances are good. Mick's related to people Dad and Mama have known for a long, long time and they both like him.

Me? I've had a crush on Mick since forever. But he never lets anybody tease me about it. He's nice that way. Sometimes I catch him looking at me out of his quiet gray eyes and I know there's a chuckle in there someplace. But he never laughs at me. He always treats me like I'm grown up, even when I need reminders. Ricochet is gentle and steady, but very, very big. I barely come up to his shoulder. I can't saddle him myself. His rig is too heavy for me to even lift. But I can get his bridle on him just fine, so I ride him bareback. My friend Bonnie does, too, even though we really aren't supposed to, leastwise not outside of the corral. Mick knows this and will probably say something to Bonnie and me when he catches us together. And he always does. It will be our one chance before he says something to our parents. He's nice that way, too. He knows we'll never break a promise to him. It's his way of keeping us from getting our necks broke doing something foolish. Like riding big horses bareback too far . . .

We finish the sandwiches but the sun isn't finished rolling towards late in the day and Mick says as much. "Well, girl—I gotta get back to work. Let's get ya up on ol' Ricochet and get ya headed back."

I don't want the visit to end. I understand and respect work, but I still ask for something I know he'll do. I stand up and grab Ricochet's bridle off the tablecloth. "Ride us up the road to the hill and back?" I beg.

Mick stands up and folds the tablecloth for me. He puts it away in my rucksack and the lemonade bottle follows fast. He looks at me and frowns a little bit, then sighs. "Okay, but not all the way to the hill—just to the China cherry tree."

I almost jump up and down. The bottom of the hill I asked for was a stretch, and I know it. But the China cherry tree! That's far enough away to maybe talk Mick into giving us a lope. He's the best rider in the world and I can't wait to get up behind him on Ricochet and take off.

I snatch up my bag and throw it in the back of the pickup. Ricochet is standing quietly in the shade, grass-fed and sleeping. Mick doesn't bother with the bridle so I lay it on top of the bag. He goes over to Ricochet and wakes him up with a couple of pats. Then he unties the lead rope. With just the rope for reins, he puts one hand on Ricochet's withers and jumps up on his back Indian style, graceful as a cat. I climb up on the back fender of the truck and wait for him to walk ol' Ricochet over. When he gets to the truck, he sidesteps him closer then reaches his arm out for me. He swings me up behind him and I wrap my arms around him tight. "Alright, girl," he says, "ya ready?"

I giggle and hold on even tighter. "Yes, yes—let's go!" I shout.

We move away from the truck and out from under the shade at a fast walk I didn't know Ricochet had. It's like riding a mountain that woke up all of a sudden. Then we fly up the road at a big, rocking lope and laugh at the wind trying to catch us.

Another Rain Poem
by Grace Ryan

the first real day of rain
is not when the grey falls
    close to earth and the sky loses
        its stark dignity
  not when the air takes on
 a name
    and headlights yell
Red at every hour
      The first real day of rain is waking
    up alone and warm
and remembering the body
that you have so long taken
        for granted
           waking up wishing
          for carnations wrapped in newspaper
      and knowing
    that they would only get wet and cold
That the hand
        carrying them would only get
    Black with ink
And that there is no hand to carry them
      No flowers to carry you either
      Inky wet newspaper-woman that you are…

Hangnails,
by Diana Carey

    Riding proudly on my finger tips.

        Surrounding my cuticles,

            Snagging my pantyhose

                Like tiny talons

                    Of Velcro.

Hangnails

    Standing up to greet

        All I shake hands with.

            Obediently falling to my every bite.

                Lovingly caressing my hands

                    Like 80 grit

                      Sandpaper.

Hangnails

Empties

by J.D. Blair

At eight-thirty Elliot pulled into Bob's Burger drive-thru and the driver in the car in front of him shot the kid taking the orders . . . a single bullet in the chin and the kid fell out of the window spilling a bag of fries and a medium drink. The shooter laid rubber all the way out of the driveway, drove over the curb and headed downtown leaving a trail of French Fries in his wake. Elliot would do without his egg on a biscuit.

The cops showed up to investigate. A detective named Bellows questioned Elliot.

"What do you know about this?"

"I don't know anything. I was next in line and I heard the kid on the intercom."

"What did he say?"

"He said good morning, what the fuck."

"What the fuck?"

"Yes."

The cop continued. "What else?"

"Nothing, I didn't hear a shot. But I saw smoke come out of the barrel of the guy's gun."

"What kind of gun?"

"I don't know guns . . . just a pistol."

Bellows' voice took on an edge, "Well, was it a large pistol or a small pistol?"

"Like I say, I don't know guns."

The cop paused to jot a note. "What kind of car was it?"

Elliot hesitated, "I don't know, a sedan of some sort. They all look alike to me."

"What about color?"

"I'm color blind," confessed Elliot, "So I'm really not sure."

"You're color blind?" Bellows was starting to get pissed. "Christ, kid, did you see anything? A license number maybe?"

Elliot took a step back, "No, it all happened too fast."

Bellows sighed, "Tell me, do you know what race this guy was?"

"It's hard to say, from the back . . . white . . . maybe Hispanic . . . I suppose he could be black."

Bellows' face was turning red. "Jesus, kid, you've been a big help. Get out of here."

Elliot headed downtown, late for work by about an hour and a half. He would grab a stale muffin out of the vending machine at the office. He punched in his boss' number on his cell phone and tried to explain his situation but his boss wasn't having any of it and launched an attack on Elliot's lateness. Larry Bertrand was typical of every overstuffed supervisor who ever chaired a meeting and Elliot thought he was wound a little too tight. He finally had taken enough.

"Bertrand you son-of-a-bitch, I'll be there when I get there and if that isn't good enough you can take the fucking job and stick it." He punched the kill button and threw the receiver in the passenger seat. The phone buzzed back to life immediately . . . he let it go.

He passed the freeway interchange and came to a stop at Birmingham and Lincoln and he noticed a clump of the city's homeless milling around on the corner. They had a kid surrounded, hounding him for a paper bag he was carrying. It was an eerie sidewalk waltz that quickly exploded into a messy drama when the kid pulled a knife from under his sports jacket and sliced at the hand of one old guy who was grabbing at the bag. Severed fingers hit the pavement still clutching at air. The kid kicked the fingers into the gutter while the stunned old man sat down in the middle of the circling winos holding his mutilated hand watching blood pump from the stumps of his fingers. Another old guy slipped in the bloody mess on the sidewalk and fell hard on his ass. The kid, still holding the knife, skewered the fleshy underarm of a third guy who grabbed the bag and ripped it open. A dozen empty glass bottles hit the pavement and shattered, becoming just one more part of the mix of old men, body parts, and blood.

The cars at the intersection sat through a green light watching the gory dance unfold just a few feet from their windshields. Finally a taxi driver bolted from his cab and headed for the mess on the corner. The kid kicked at the torn bag at his feet and took off and disappeared into a maze of stacked pallets, boxes, and debris.

Elliot took the next green light wondering how much you could get for an empty. Two cents? A nickel? They're cutting off fingers over empties? His thoughts deflected back to when he collected empties as a kid just to get the fifty cents for the movies on Saturday afternoon, the challenge of collecting the bottles, the art of collecting only the most valuable. Today empties are a precious barter item on the screwy black market of the streets. Would he give up a body part for an empty? He recalled the fist fights over discarded milk bottles and empty soft drink bottles and irate name calling . . . the fury of those who had and those who didn't. The only real difference he decided is that they didn't carry weapons.

Elliot continued downtown and for several blocks a red pickup followed him with a black girl at the wheel and a white guy in the passenger seat. She was attractive, primitive looking, with beads laced closely around her neck and rings on her fingers that caught the sun as she gestured toward her passenger. He was average looking except for the earring in his left lobe. He had a goatee and was wearing dark glasses. They were in the middle of an argument and the action began to heat up when he started waving a pistol in the girl's face.

Traffic stopped at Lincoln and Stoll Avenue and Elliot's eyes were locked on his rear view mirror. The girl shoved the guy's shoulder trying to push him to the other side of the truck cab. He was waving the gun around laughing and she finally slugged him on the cheek, hitting him so hard his dark glasses flew into the windshield. He shook it off and retaliated by whipping her with the pistol, spinning her head into the side window. A gash opened up under her right eye, along the cheekbone, like a boxer's cut. She slumped over the steering wheel and the guy opened her door and shoved her into the street. She tumbled onto the road like a sack of potatoes and rolled onto the median with her colorful caftan bunched up around her waist. The guy slid behind the wheel and was still shouting at her when the light changed. The girl was on all fours floundering like a struck animal, her face bleeding as she struggled to get up. Nobody stopped to help her, the traffic stream got anxious and hurried on through the intersection when the light turned. When Elliot turned his attention back to the truck, it was gone.

Elliot was ready to call Bertrand to tell him he wouldn't be in at all, but he wasn't up to listening to any more of his philosophy on being punctual and maintaining a professional profile. Screw professional, people are killing each other, fighting over empty glass and a woman is bleeding in the street after being pistol-whipped. He'd go to work just to get off the streets.

He cruised through the busy downtown as delivery trucks clogged the streets and shops began to open. He checked to make sure his doors were locked, windows rolled up. He tried to hit all the lights not wanting to stop, become a target. He breathed a small and short-lived sigh of relief as his building came into view.

Before he could make the turn into the garage, a paramedic's ambulance careened past him on the left, swerved in front of him and sped into the garage ahead of him. He followed it in and the two vehicles spiraled down three levels into the bowels of the Altman Building, home to Brookings Finance. He was searching for a parking space when out of the dark corners of the garage a SWAT team materialized and surrounded his car. They were all aiming automatic weapons . . . at him.

"Out of the car . . . slowly," shouted a cop standing at the left rear fender. Elliot could see him in the mirror, the rifle pointing at Elliot's head. He got out of the car to face the muzzle of the rifle.

"Both hands on top of the car . . . slowly."

Elliot assumed the position and a flurry of blue surrounded him and before he knew it he was searched and cuffed. A voice came from the darkness, behind the line of police. "What's your name?"

"Elliot Bonner," his voice quivered. "I work on the fifth floor, Brookings Finance. What's going on?"

"I'll ask the questions." The man behind the voice appeared out of the group of cops. Pickens was the name on his badge plate. "What do you do at Brookings?"

"I'm a mortgage officer. I work for Mr. Bertrand, Larry Bertrand."

"Really. Have you worked for Mr. Bertrand long?"

"About two years. Call him, he'll tell you."

Pickens stepped close to Elliot. "Well Elliott, we've got a small problem." He unlocked the cuffs and turned Elliot around to face him. "I'd love to talk to Mr. Bertrand, but it seems he went a little crazy in the office with a pistol this morning. He took out a secretary and two security guards then stuck the gun barrel up his nose and blew his brains out."

"What?" Elliot couldn't decipher what Pickens was telling him. The words couldn't find a spot alongside the other messy episodes that had taken place that morning.

Pickens continued. "Do you know any reason why Bertrand would go off like that?"

There was a long pause in the deathly quiet of the garage. Elliot stared in disbelief at the detective.

"Well?" asked Pickens.

"I was late to work?" Elliot whispered.

"What?"

"I was late for work?"

The following day, Roland Endorain sat slumped in a back booth at Nick's bar cradling his bandaged hand across his chest. He had lost the battle over the bag of empty bottles and two fingers on his left hand were gone down to the second knuckle, a third lost the tip. Rollo, as he was known on the street, hugged the shadows that spread across the wall in a mottled mosaic. He ducked a shaft of late afternoon sunlight kicking up dust particles over his left shoulder. He was in pain and the brandy wasn't helping.

"Rollo, you want another?" Nick leaned over the bar trying to get the old guy's attention. "Hey Rollo, Rollo, another drink?"

Rollo turned his ruddy face toward Nick but said nothing. Nick took that as a "yes" and poured another and nodded to the fat barmaid Bea to deliver it. Drinks marked the passage of time for the old man and four empties were lined up at his undamaged right hand. Bea brought the drink and stood by as Rollo took it all with a quick swallow. He turned toward Bea and raised the injured hand, his face etched in pain. "Why, Bea?"

"No reason to it, Rollo, no reason."

Rollo picked at the bandaged hand, "I needed the empties, I got more need of them than him."

"It ain't a question of need, I guess," said Bea. "I think it's whose got 'em first." Bea moved on, leaving the old man to his pain.

Rollo lived day-to-day on the street. He came to the bar every day except Sunday. Sundays he spent in silent remembrance of his family, long dead. Six yellowing family photographs and a worn strand of rosary beads were his only possessions. On Sundays, in his penance, Rollo faced the reality of his loneliness without liquor.

"You don't want to look into his eyes," warned Nick, popping a stale peanut into his mouth.

"The old guy's sort of spooky," said Bea.

"It's guilt."

"Guilt, what's he got to be guilty about?"

"Over being alive." Nick tossed another peanut.

Rollo heard their conversation, but ignored it and continued to stare at the wall as he rocked back and forth counting each painful throb shooting into his damaged hand.

As the afternoon moved into evening the Saturday night regulars began to arrive, mostly young, boisterous types, blowing off a week's worth of frustration. They all knew Rollo, but never bothered to pay him much attention. This evening things were different. Word was around the old guy had a run-in with some punk over empties and was hurting.

"Hey old man, you need a bodyguard?" shouted a guy in a hard hat.

"Rollo, how's it goin' man?" asked another, patting the old man's shoulder as he passed the booth.

A couple of guys sat down across from Rollo, ordering up brandy for him and making small talk.

Throughout the evening nearly everyone touched the old man. Rollo, bewildered by the attention, spoke very little. As the evening wore on everyone left empty bottles on his table. When someone would stop to say hello another empty would be added to the dozen or so already crowding the booth.

The Saturday night crowd partied around the old man into the following day. At two-thirty in the morning on Sunday, the bar had emptied. Bea was gone and only the whir of a ventilator fan cut the silence as Nick prepared to close up. In the crush of business, he had forgotten about Rollo, and in making a final check of the bar, he noticed the old man in his booth surrounded by empties. There must have been a hundred or so . . . beer bottles, shot glasses and mugs. Rollo was slumped over the table, face down with his bandaged hand held behind his head with the rosary dangling from his swollen thumb.

Nick tried to wake the old guy, but when he couldn't, he realized he had served him for the last time.

"I guess he just gave up," Nick said to the ambulance attendants.

Rollo's Sunday family reunion would take place as usual.

With long, smooth strokes Poco Sanchez was sharpening his knife, pulling the blade across a small polishing stone. Poco just turned fifteen, the youngest and newest member of the "Zapatas." He had yet to earn his stripes with the gang and knifing old winos over empties wasn't going to get it done. Taunts from other gang members were relentless.

"Poco, pricked any winos today?"

"What's next Poco, old ladies?"

"You can't hold onto empties, Poco? My baby sister could hold 'em against winos."

Poco sheathed the knife and shuffled out of the alley, away from the jibes. Throughout the afternoon he wandered the neighborhood. A trio of brothers was gathered on the corner of Birmingham and Madison, across from Nick's Bar. Rico, Pablo and Santos were the top officers of the gang. They were hanging out with their ladies, drinking beer.

Poco approached, "Hey guys, what's happening?"

Conversation among the group stopped as the kid walked up. They looked at each other and their ladies stepped away.

Poco tried again, "Rico, Santos, where's the action?"

Santos spoke up. "Action, Poco? You're sure you want action? Seems like you got all the action you can handle, little brother."

"You mean the wino? No problem with that man, I handled it."

"You handled it? You killed the old gringo, Poco."

Poco hadn't heard about Rollo's death. He looked at each of them in turn not sure of how to respond.

Rico nodded towards Nick's bar. "They carried him out of there this morning. The old wino's dead."

Poco spoke up, "I didn't kill the old man, just cut off some fingers. Besides, they was taking my stuff."

"I don't care what you say kid, people are gonna think you killed the old guy and the rest of us are gonna pay."

"I ain't takin' a fall for this shit, man," Poco stepped back and his hand went to the knife grip.

He didn't want to earn his stripes against a brother, but he would if he had to.

Rico stepped forward. "Hey, little brother, you aren't gonna pull down on me are you?"

Poco's palm was slippery on the knife handle. "I didn't kill that old wino Rico. I didn't kill nobody."

"Give me the blade, Poco. I'll hold it 'til you get your stripes."

Sunlight flickered off the blade as Poco drew the knife. He held it up between them. He had no intention of handing it over. "You'll have to take it from me."

"You don't want this, Poco," said Rico, "you ain't up to it. Give me the blade."

Rico made a slow move toward Poco's hand and the blade slashed out, grazing Rico's forearm. Rico's jaw tightened. Any slack he was willing to give Poco was disappearing. He glanced at his arm, no blood. He took another step. "No blood, no damage, no problem. Give me the blade."

Poco shifted his balance as Rico approached. Rico made a quick grab for the knife but Poco ducked under Rico's arm and nicked his elbow. A ribbon of red slid down Rico's arm. His short fuse ran its course and he picked up an empty beer bottle and shortened it against a stop sign. He held it up, jagged butt toward Poco. "You're makin' a big fuckin' mistake, kid. Give me the blade and this ends right here."

Poco's heart was in his throat and his knees were rubber. He had pushed too far and he couldn't back down. "I can't give up my blade, Rico."

"You ain't gonna make your stripes on me, little brother."

A quick thrust of the broken empty caught Poco off guard. A cut opened up along his cheek. He tasted blood as it slipped to his lips.

"Now, give me the blade, Poco." Rico advanced on the youngster and Poco backed up.

Tears filled Poco's eyes. "No." He lunged to score on Rico's shoulder, but missed, leaving him vulnerable. The jagged glass ripped into Poco's throat under his right ear and caught an artery. Blood drenched his shirt before he hit the sidewalk. Rico knew he had killed the kid and stood over Poco, crossed himself and dropped the beer bottle at his feet. He walked away and the others followed slowly behind.

Shawna Draper spent Friday and Saturday night at her sister's place. She hadn't talked to Cliff since he kicked her into the street on Friday. As usual it was a stupid argument about work. Cliff, an undercover narcotics cop led two incompatible lives, one in the streets, and the other in the comfort of the apartment he shared with Shawna. He brought too much of the streets into their home.

The apartment was dark when she got home on Sunday, only the glow of the television screen flickered from the living room. She turned on the bathroom light to survey the damage done in the fight. A butterfly bandage bridged four stitches under her blackened right eye. There were scrapes on her left elbow and both knees where she met the road. On the bathroom mirror was a note from Cliff. In a drunken scrawl he wrote that he was tired of fighting. It went on about how he couldn't go on hurting her and how he couldn't seem not to hurt her. It was a letter full of pain and boozy ramblings that didn't make much sense.

Shawna headed down the hall to the living room that smelled of popcorn and whisky. Cliff was passed out on the couch. His police issue pistol, an empty clip and unspent slugs were scattered on the coffee table. She picked up the gun and turned off the TV.

"Cliff," she whispered. "Cliff, wake up." She knelt next to him and as she often did to wake him, tugged on his earring. Cliff stirred but didn't rouse from his stupor.

"Cliff, come on, wake up." She gave another tug on his ear.

"What," Cliff mumbled, "what time is it?"

"It's Sunday night, eight o'clock. I'm going to turn on the light."

"No Shawna, don't. Leave it off. Where you been?"

"Elaine's. I was afraid to come home."

Cliff reached out in the darkness and his hand brushed the gun barrel. "Hey, what have you got there?"

In the darkness she moved the gun forward and nudged it under Cliff's chin. "It's your gun."

Cliff stiffened as the cold metal settled against his skin. "Don't play around Shawna, use your head."

"I'm not playing around and I am using my head. We're going to settle things here and now."

"But this isn't the answer, Hon. Let's talk this out."

"I've tried talking but you never listen. I guess this is the only way to settle it."

Shawna put both hands on the gun and as she did it pulled away enough for Cliff to wrench it from her. From the weight of the piece Cliff could tell it wasn't loaded. He turned on the lamp and cleared the chamber to verify it. Shawna was sheepishly cowering in the corner of the couch. Her impish grin gave away the charade.

Cliff shook his head, "You little phony."

"I had to get your attention."

"You could always kick me out of a truck."

"That's not funny, Cliff."

"No, it's not," he admitted, "I'm sorry, baby, I'm so sorry."

Shawna had heard the words before but this time they seemed to have a ring of truth in them. There was reason, for the moment anyway, to think they would survive their latest brutal exchange.

They settled in for the night sharing the couch, watching the news. The lead story was about some guy going berserk in a financial office and killing three people, then blowing his brains out.

"Christ," said Cliff, "what would make a guy do that?"

caught up

by sandra kay

    i like to get caught up
    thinkin' 'bout
    thinkin' 'bout
    bein' thought of
    i like to think 'bout
    bein' thought of
    bein' thought of
    by you

    and i wonder if you ever get caught up

    wonderin' 'bout
    wonderin' 'bout
    whether
    if you ever get caught
    wonderin'
    whether i'm thinkin'
    'bout you?

Speed of Life
by Kathy Mima

Wind sock dangles
its ten | ta | cles
like an oc | to | pus
washed-out green
like the forest
brown amber rust-colored
ferns from last year
ferns from this
   Dap pled
    tree trunks
grey tan brown
      bark
dap pled moss
lime pale green
   dap pled
     sun light
  sun light
warm…
bringing up the juices
blackberry leaves scent
the air blending cricket and crow
with silence.

The world is silenced.
Forest rushes by—a sound so full
of Quiet

Tree tops catch the wind

and roots hold
the earth
still.

Last Revolutionary War Widow Dies

by David Hardiman

Framingham MA—Lucretia Goodshoes a.k.a Anna-Nicole Goodshoes, the last surviving Revolutionary War widow, died Saturday at the Framingham Convalescent Home for the Seriously Aged. Mrs. Goodshoes' cause of death was desiccation. "She simply dried out," said the home's director, Sylvia Nethercutt.

In a freakish convergence of super longevity and improbable mathematics, Lucretia, or "Crete," as she was known, became the unlikely widow of fabled Revolutionary War veteran Ezekiel Goodshoes. During her long life spanning one entire century and parts of two others, she collected more than fifteen million dollars in federal pensions as General Goodshoes' rightful widow. Incredibly, this is more money than the Continental Congress spent in fighting the entire Revolutionary War. As most recall from their school textbooks, Ezekiel served as a ten-year old powder monkey under General Washington at the final battle and British surrender of Yorktown, October 19, 1781. Despite a withering British bombardment, young Ezekiel brought badly needed gunpowder to Lt. Colonel Alexander Hamilton at redoubt number ten ensuring a successful siege and winning praise from no less than General Washington himself: "It is expendable orphaned street urchins like Private Goodshoes that made our victory possible."

In 1889, at the age of one, Mrs. Goodshoes (born Lucretia Tattersoul) was wedded to then 118-year-old General in an arranged marriage that took place in the Territory of Oklahoma where marrying out of your century was perfectly legal. Her father, Greenspan Tattersoul, an annuity salesman who knew the value of a steady pension, arranged the marriage.

They honeymooned in the nursery where Ezekiel died getting out of the crib the next morning when he tripped on the railing and hit his head on a maypole. "Crete" loved Ezekiel and vowed to never marry again in order to honor his legacy and, more importantly, to ensure she'd collect on the hefty pension he left her. Instead of remarrying, she lived with a succession of caring and compassionate "uncles." She mourned the loss of her husband with ferocious grief. And as was the custom of the day she dressed in black for the remainder of the nineteenth century, throughout the twentieth century and on into the twenty-first century. In her memoir, *I Don't Give a Continental*, a defiant Crete discussed the fond memories of her late husband:

"He wasn't so much a father figure as he was a great-great-great grandfather figure. We had such plans. He was going to whittle me a series of nesting Presidential dolls. Like those Russian kachina dolls. He was gonna carve me US Grant all the way through to Grover Cleveland. Wouldn't carve that scoundrel Garfield though because, 'he's all mixed up in that Credit Mobilier railroad scandal don't you know. Pawn of JP Morgan and Cornelius Vanderbilt he is. Give me a Polk or a Pierce any day. Now thems was Presidents.'

"Oh he was so thoughtful on our wedding day. At the altar he gave me a diamond rattle he did. Our honeymoon was cut short by the crib incident, but I fondly recall Ezekiel bouncing me on his bony knee and the charming stench of his ancient colonial breath. The way he placed the bottle in my mouth and smiled with those glistening rheumy eyes of his, you could tell he had taken a shine to me. He had thick tufts of hair growing out of most every place but his head. Some said it wouldn't work 'cuz it's an early-spring late-winter romance, but theys was wrong. It was good infantile love what we's had and everybody knew it. There was no funny business neither. He was going to stay chaste till I was eighteen which would've put him at 135. Men slow down then y'see. Usually to a screechin' halt. Anyhoo my Ezekiel got me a pink ribbon once. Said someday they'd all be wearin'em for breast awareness day. I don't give a continental what they say—we was in love."

General Goodshoes had a long and storied Army career. For his exploits in the Revolutionary War he was awarded 1200 acres of land in the Northwest Territory in an area that eventually became Lake Michigan. Later on as a General in the War of 1812 he served with great extinction. During the Civil War (1861-65) the doddering general became disoriented and fought for the West. By the time he met "Crete" in 1889 he was ready to settle down. Throughout their brief courtship he would bring her wooden blocks and she'd give him spittle. By his third date the 118-year-old General properly asked her 24-year-old father for her hand in marriage. Mr. Tattersoul mulled it over and said, "Well OK. But you can't just take her hand. You've got to take the whole person. You are still getting that pension aren't you?"

"Every two weeks whether I want it or not. It's as regular as a McCormick Reaper," General Goodshoes responded.

All eyes turned expectantly toward Lucretia awaiting her answer. She cooed, "Birdy num-num," which her father quickly interpreted for everyone as, "Yes. Let's marry immediately."

A Cherokee shaman performed the ceremony that afternoon and they enjoyed seventeen hours of uninterrupted domestic bliss.

Due to a threshing machine accident in her youth in which her foot was briefly separated from the chaff, Lucretia walked with a decided limp and when later asked what she treasured in life, she responded, "Goodshoes. It's all about Goodshoes." In her final moments she expressed dismay that Ezekiel had missed her previous 117 birthdays. Her last words were, 'Is this the end of num-num'?

Mrs. Goodshoes is survived by her older sister Delilah, who is still collecting a British pension for services her dearly departed husband, Major Percival Dinwiddie, rendered in the French and Indian War of 1754-60.

The Chair

excerpted from a longer story
by Selene Steese

The thing gave him the willies. He didn't know where the Simonson's had gotten it, but he remembered when they'd first brought the damn thing home. Huffing and puffing, Mr. Simonson had carried it up the stairs to the third floor and set it in an alcove near the landing. Edgar had come upon it later that same day, as he was seeing to his regular duties.

He'd been humming away happily as he ran the Handi-Vac over one section of runner, then the next. He had finished with the plush royal blue runners on the second floor stairs and was three-quarters of the way up the forest green runners on the third-floor staircase when he felt it—a prickle at the back of his neck. He was facing east, because he remembered the sun spreading its first buttery rays above the hills. All the picture windows had been installed on the east side of the house just for that green, rolling view. So while his front felt warm and glowy, his back felt cold and goose bumpy. He was absolutely certain he was being watched, but he knew that Mr. Simonson was on the first floor, in the kitchen making sausage and eggs, and that Mrs. Simonson was in the second floor bathroom taking a shower. He was the only person on the third floor.

Edgar had turned around slowly, reluctant to pull away from that bright warmth. He sucked his breath in sharp when he saw it—that damn chair.

It was clearly an antique. They hadn't made wheelchairs like that in nearly a century. Tucked into a corner, the chair was half-entombed in shadow. The parts he could make out were painted a rusty, unhealthy shade of orange. The wheels—big things with about a thousand spokes—looked like they'd been pilfered from a highboy, one of those old-fashioned bicycles. Looking at the chair, Edgar was certain that the sun would not be able to reveal all of it—that even if the sun came close enough to the Earth to flash fry him where he stood, all that candle power still could not show the chair in its entirety.

No, Edgar did not like the chair, but what disturbed him most about it was its . . . well, its presence. That was the only way he could think of to describe the sense of expectant dread he felt each time he saw it. And he got to see it a lot. Unfortunately for him, Mr. Simonson had decided to ensconce the thing on the third floor, the same floor where Edgar had his sleeping quarters. Edgar had thought about asking to move his quarters to the second or first floor—even the basement. He had tried to have this conversation just once with Mr. Simonson, and once was quite enough.

He had walked into Mr. Simonson's study, hat in hand, smoothing back his dark, bristly hair.

"Uh, 'scuse me Mr. Simonson, sir, but I'd like to talk to you about changing my sleeping quarters."

Mr. Simonson had looked up from a stack of papers on his desk with a gusty sigh.

"Why do you want to do that?" he said, his gaze straying back to the papers.

"Well, sir, I . . . you see, it's . . . well, sir, to be honest as I know how, it's that chair," Edgar had stammered out, turning his cap over and over in his hands.

Mr. Simonson had stared hard at him then, papers forgotten for the moment.

"Chair? What chair? What are you on about, Edgar?"

Edgar had felt his shoulders slump, his head bowing almost of its own accord. He'd swallowed hard and somehow gotten out the next few words.

"Th-that old one on the third floor—the wheelchair."

Mr. Simonson had glared at Edgar over the top of his reading glasses, face getting redder by the moment.

"What about it? It's a valuable antique. Mrs. Simonson was quite taken with it, so we decided to add it to our collection. There isn't anything wrong with it, I hope?"

Then Mrs. Simonson had come into the study, rescuing him from further humiliation. He remembered she'd been wiping her delicate, long-fingered hands on a blue-and-white-checked dishtowel.

"What is all the fuss about in here?" she had said, crossing the room to stand near Mr. Simonson. "Why are you raising your voice, Ben? You know what Dr. Wexler said about overexciting yourself."

Then she had fixed Mr. Simonson with a stern but loving gaze, the sort of look that Edgar often wished she would turn on him.

"Yes, yes, I know," Mr. Simonson had said. "Honestly, Rose, there's no need to treat me like a child."

Rosamund Simonson had smiled indulgently and stroked her husband's hair, silver-white beneath her beautiful hands. Then she turned her gaze, soft but with no love in it, upon Edgar.

"Run along now," she said, her voice carrying a chill to rival the early March winds rattling the windows of the study. "I'm sure you have work to do."

Edgar had turned away real quick, before she could see the longing in his eyes. She was never what you would call warm toward him, but he loved his Rosamund just the same.

No, it was a conversation he was never going to repeat. So, he continued to live on the third floor, passing within reach (that was the way he thought of it—as though the thing might roll out and grab at him) of the chair about a dozen times a day. But as bad as the days were, the nights were much worse.

Edgar would lie awake most nights until exhaustion overtook him. Then he'd have extraordinarily vivid dreams, always featuring the chair. In one, the chair would move on its own, slowly, creakily rolling across the third floor's forest green hall carpet until it sat just outside Edgar's door—empty and waiting. He would wake from this dream in a sweat and run to the door of his quarters, yank it open and find—a quiet, shadow-and-moonlight painted hallway. He'd walk over to where the chair lived (he had come to regard it as a living thing) and it would always be ensconced in its realm of deep shadow, made depthless by the night.

The most awful dream, though, was the one about the chair and Mrs. Simonson. He always woke from that one with a strangled cry and tears on his cheeks. Then he had to creep down to the second floor and put his ear against the door of the Simonson's bedroom. He would listen, sometimes for an hour or more, until he was sure he could hear the soprano notes of Rosamund's snores in the lull between the *basso profundo* snores that came from Mr. Simonson. Only then would he stop trembling; only then would his tears cease.

That dream began in the Simonson's orchard. They didn't really have one now, but he'd heard there had been a grove of ancient peach and plum trees on this land when they'd first moved here. In his dream, though, the orchard is alive and thriving, the trees both heavy with fruit and bursting with blossoms—something Edgar knows is impossible, but then, this is a dream.

Rosamund Simonson is dancing in the midst of the orchard, wearing a gown of diaphanous (and nearly transparent) white. Around her drifts a shower of peach and plum blossoms, and she puts to shame their soft, pastel beauty. Her long, silver-white hair shines and flows and she spins and dances, spins and dances, spins and dances and begins to bleed.

The first wound appears above one of her perfect, kissable, plum-sized breasts—Edgar can see the rosy nipple so clearly through the white dress. Blood wells, rich and hot and shockingly red against the whiteness of her gown, her beautiful breast. Then a wound appears on her lovely face, along the right side of her head. This injury looks like the imprint of a bloody boot.

He tries to run to her as she spins and bleeds and screams, he tries to run but the branches hold him, the branches upon which the blossoms are now withering, crisping from pink to brown, then to black. The branches twist around his arms, hold him back from helping her. It is at this point in the dream, when he is held captive and his attention is fixed, that he first notices the chair.

In this dream it looks different—darker, not that horrid shade of sickroom orange. It is sitting at the entrance to the orchard and he can just make it out through the long corridor formed by withering plum and peach trees.

He struggles even more valiantly to free himself from the grip of the dead branches, and this time he succeeds. He runs toward Rosamund, who seems farther away than she should be. The distance between them expands and he sees her collapse to the blossom-littered earth, her gown more red than white, her hair, too, liberally painted with blood.

When he reaches her still form, he bends down to gather her bleeding body in his arms. But he gathers only red-stained white cloth—Rosamund's remains are not within. Then, he hears it—that dreaded, dreadful squeaking of ancient metal wheels. He turns, the white-and-blood dress still clutched in his hands, and there is his Rosamund—naked, dead, and sitting in the chair. She regards him through eyes covered with a milky film. Then she smiles, revealing rows of needle-sharp teeth, and beckons him forward.

This is always the point at which he wakes, bedclothes bunched in his hands as though he still grasped Rosamund's beautiful, ruined dress.

After several weeks of such dreams, Rosamund comes across him one day on the second floor. He is leaning against the wall, eyes closed, trying to catch his breath. She looks at him from eyes thickly ringed with purplish blue. Her lovely face is haggard, and when she sees the same bruised eyes and haggard look on Edgar's face, she turns away to stop him from seeing the widening of her eyes, the trembling of her lower lip. Then she looks back because she can't help herself, and his eyes are open.

He knows! She thinks. He knows about the dreams!

Edgar, who had opened his eyes in time to see her turn away, can hardly believe it.

She knows! He thinks. But how can she? Unless. . .

He looks at her, amazed, and she looks at him, alarmed.

Are we both having the same dreams? Thinks Edgar.

Rosamund starts as though he said this aloud—and perhaps he did. These days, he is sure of very little that he does or says. Sure of little except of that which he is always sure—that he loves her unreservedly.

"Are you all right?" he says, this time reasonably certain he is speaking aloud.

Rosamund begins to back away from him, shaking her head.

"Stay away from me," she whispers. "Keep back."

"But I. . ." he says, taking a step forward.

Rosamund turns and tries to run down the stairs, nearly falls. When she rights herself, she glares at him as though he caused all this—her mishap just now, the terrible dreams, her fights with Ben, her trouble sleeping.

"Just keep away from me," she hisses.

Then she runs, runs, runs down the third floor stairs, down the second floor stairs and as she runs, Edgar is calling after her, calling, saying something that makes no sense.

"The chair," he calls. "It's the chair. This is all because of the chair."

And that is how Rosamund Simonson, who (Dr. Wexler admonished) at the age of 58 should know better than to run down three flights of stairs without some sort of warm up (she told him she was exercising) ended up with an injured right ankle and (at Mr. Simonson's insistence) in the chair.

Creature from the Black Lagoon
by Charan Sue Wollard

The beast slithers deep
beneath brackish water.
How many heads does it possess?
How many teeth in every head?
How many red eyes rip like razors
through the dark lagoon?
Rapacious tentacles thrash, parry,
its intentions clear.
Yet even a beast's aortic rhythms sync
with whatever flailing prey
it devours.

Saturday Evening in Harvard Square

by Grace Ryan

latenight taps
of treasured heels
heads folded one over the other
conniving
wet whispers slathered in whiskey
vodka
Whateverwasfreetonight
and the lazy arms cloaking shoulder bones
stroking collar bones
looking for bones on the ice-glazed streets
vagrant, untenable streets
    we all need a little foundation sometimes
    and a little freedom
    but you, you are making a pilgrimage for which there is no name,
    and I, well I'm simply returning home
    to the rattling dry bones of a room worth forgetting
    the room of an unhappy monk who dreams of escape all night
    and throws stones at the birds
    in the morning

Voice Voyage
by Tom Darter

I seem to be a vessel;
I try to hold as much as I can.

I know I'll be scooped out in the end
    (all those preciously saved things gone);
but, until then, I want to keep adding more, doing more.

I'm finally finding freedom
    in the use of this vessel on stage.
It feels good; and, wonder of wonders:

This new looseness,
    discovered in a refound passion,
has given me a new freedom,
    a new looseness,
in my first language.

Seated at the piano now,
    I dance in place,
finally free to simply feel the music
    flowing through my fingers.
My body becomes part of the music.

I guess I've finally given myself permission
    (both within and without)
to enjoy what I can do.

And, you know, most of the time
I don't even worry about looking silly.

It feels so good to feel loose onstage.

And it feels so good to feel loose at the piano;
    to feel (with my whole body)
the music I'm playing.

To be able to feel with my entire vessel,
    not with just my head.

Finally, I am sailing.

The Unannounced Visitor

by Karen L. Hogan

I stopped writing
Because I didn't know what to say,
Stopped in mid-sentence by my mother's death.

It wasn't grief as you'd expect:
    A dark pool of emptiness;
    Of missing her;
    Of cursing death.

No.
Grief would arrive unannounced,
A rogue wave pulling me from what I hoped would be,
Carrying me to a riptide of words half-said—
The undertow calling me
To drown in an ocean of unrequited love.

In the end,
I would
save
my self,
Swimming with the tide until I could say the unsaid:

    I forgive us,
    For we are spirits
    learning
    to be human.

And, then, I would wash ashore,
Miles from where Grief pulled me away.

Why I Write, Part III

by Selene Steese

I write to move the Earth beneath
my feet, to cause upheaval. To spare
myself the pain, then bring it
back and back and back. I write

I write to bite back at life, to chew,
to swallow, to digest all that the world
lays at my feet.

I write to stop making sense, to stomp
on logic and hold obligation
in a hammerlock. I write

to be a pain in the ass, to swipe
my wicked wit through the debit slot
of life, to boogie down with the mechanized
demons who have stolen
this millennium's soul. I write

to sprint along the asphalt of paved-over
dreams, to pick fleshy nightmare flowers,
purple as a bruise. I write

to stumble, to fall, to get back up
and thumb my nose at the bump
in the road. I write

to be the princess who kissed toad
and liked it, who licked the bumpy
back of a hallucinogenic toad
and took a trip, man, if you
know what I mean. I write

to see things I ain't never seen, things
I ain't gonna see any other way. I write

to fool around with work and get
dead serious about play. To build palaces
from Legos and Lincoln Logs
that families of twenty four can live in
with room to spare. I write

to wonder at dinky little Lincoln Logs
being any legacy of a great man,
to wonder what he thinks of that, if he's
in a position to know, a position that's not
prone and rolling over and over and over
in his grave. I write

to see how much more of this
I can come up with, to find out if
the fount is dry, or if it ever will be. I write

to rediscover that it's not likely I could ever stop,
even if I wanted to. Even if this piece
was really, really bugging you and you could
only find peace if I would shut the hell up. I write

to tell you to plug your ears, because
that just ain't gonna happen,
no way, no how. I write

to take to task the politicians, to break the backs
of their rat-bastard rules, to say "Repeal
the writ of war, you mongers
who hunger for it so." I write
to say "Hell, no, I won't go." I write
to say "Hell, yes, I will go—on and on and on
and on until all pens run out of ink,
until both hands run out of uncramped
muscles, until my heart
runs
down.

I write.

Anthology Contributors

Ian Ray Armkchnet — Ian Ray Armknecht moved to Livermore against his will after being press-ganged by his relatives to get the hell out of Seattle. His inspiration comes from walking everywhere with his head down and forgetting his headphones. He cannot think of an additional fourteen words, so this will have to do.

J.D. Blair — J. D. Blair writes short fiction, poetry, and essays. His story "Downer" will appear in *Orchid: A Literary Review* where it won their short, short fiction competition for pieces under a thousand words. A short story "Charlotta's Wake" appeared in the recent issue of *Homestead Review*. He lives in Walnut Creek.

Diana Carey — Diana Carey lives in Livermore with her husband and two dogs. She writes for fun and has been writing for about four years. Diana also enjoys carving stone pendants, which she sells at the LAA Art Gallery on 3rd Street in Livermore.

David Collins — David writes novels, short stories, monologues, and poetry. Recently, he writes about getting old, running away, and the goals he surrendered. A native Texan currently working on a coming-of-middle-age novel, David woke one morning and realized that he had spent half his life in California. He hasn't been the same since.

Pat Coyle — Pat Coyle grew up on ranches along the front range of the Rockies and around his grandparent's plumbing business in Santa Fe. He's worked as a programmer, on a ranch development in Belize, and as an engineer. He and his wife live in Livermore and have two grown children.

Tom Darter — A musician and actor who also writes words, Tom was the founding editor of *Keyboard* magazine. He has appeared in Shakesepeare Associates' and Las Positas' productions. His *One-Step (At a Time) Rag*, a one-movement concerto in ragtime for piano and orchestra, premiered on October 13, 2007 at the Bankhead Theater in Livermore.

Harold Gower — Born in Reno, and raised in Winnemucca, Nevada, Harold Gower spent much of his young life in the rural setting of the Great Basin. His first publication, *Watershed a Great Basin Epiphany*, contains nearly 100 poems describing his early impressions, and has many examples of various forms of poetry.

Jason Hambrecht — Jason Hambrecht is an exogenous Californian inhabiting Livermore's dust-and-tumble westside. Mister Hambrecht consistently appears on *People*'s Most Eligible Bachelor list. Check near the back of the unabridged edition. Last page. Second from the bottom. Call me!

David Hardiman — While not being typecast as the lead in movies about God, Mr. Hardiman enjoys making noise in his quiet moments7 Although never attending or graduating Harvard, he has a deep appreciation for Ivy League cafeteria workers7 He expresses this by ending all his sentences with the number 7

Bryant Hoex   A Bay Area native with BAs in Theatre and English from Santa Clara University, Bryant teaches and directs school plays in Dublin, and performs in Livermore Shakespeare Festival productions. He thanks Karen Hogan for supporting his writing and invites readers to contact him at bhoex@hotmail.com with responses to his story.

Karen Hogan   Karen writes short stories, monologues, essays, and poems. She is currently working on a novel. The Faulkner quote, an excerpt from his Nobel Prize speech, installed at the perforoming arts plaza was inspired by her 2005 proposal to the Commission for the Arts. She founded Saturday Salons at 4th Street Studio in 2004.

Ben Jones   Ben Jones is working his way through MFT night school by working days as a software engineer in a biotechnology firm. He loves biology, gardening, writing, and thinking about the mysteries of life.

sandra kay   blogger * poet * speaker * writing coach * artist * future playwright. posts randomly here: shesayswithasmile.blogspot.com. comments consistently here: leonardstegmann.blogspot.com. drives in the slow lane, reads in the park, writes where she is. lives in pleasanton with two children, two plants, one old, old, computer.

Bobbie Kinkead   Story is her life says Bobbie Kinkead. From her education in dramatic Colorado, to school teaching in frontier Alaska, and then nesting with her family in the diversified Bay Area, she has practiced writing and illustrating. As teacher, mother, artist, author, and storyteller she now creates stories for others to enjoy.

Jennifer Lock   Jennifer grew up in the Midwest and moved to the Bay Area in 2003. She has been writing poetry for over twenty years. In her recent work she is exploring the "stories" of her youth and retelling them as she thinks they should be told.

Susan Mayall   Born in 1933 in England, Susan Mayall's memories of a wartime childhood in idyllic surroundings dominate her writing, despite an eventful life since: Cambridge University and meeting her husband—moves to Canada, Philadelphia, and Livermore—raising four children—teaching history, running Goodenough Books—hiking, skiing, traveling, —protesting wars.

Ethel Mays   San Francisco resident Ethel Mays grew up in Tulare County where Sierra Nevada foothills protect pockets of unspoiled open range. Her writing is in Canadian and U.S. publications and she reads regularly at the San Francisco Writers Workshop.

Kathy Mima   Kathy Mima recently started attending Saturday Salons. She credits her parents for infusing her childhood with a love of stories. With an M.A. in psychology, she enjoys teaching and counseling. Kathy is currently working on a book about her spiritual journey to the Southwest. This is her first anthology appearance.

Cynthia Patton   Cynthia Patton has worked as an environmental attorney, technical editor, and nonprofit advocate—and still doesn't know what to be when she grows up. A Livermore native, she returned home in 1993 and has one daughter. Cynthia's nonfiction appears in newspapers, magazines, and several books. She's currently writing a memoir.

Kelly Pollard   Kelly Pollard is a busy mother of two and writes regularly for *Bay Area Parent* and *Contra Costa Times*. She is also the Suburban Queen columnist for *Valley Lifestyles* magazine. She is currently searching for an agent and publisher for her young adult novel.

Timothy B. Rien — Timothy B. Rien is a practicing criminal defense attorney with offices in Livermore. He received post-graduate training in creative writing at Harvard University, the Iowa Writers' Workshop, University of Iowa, and completed studies for his Master of Fine Arts degree in writing at the University of San Francisco.

Grace Ryan — Grace Ryan is a Livermore-born eccentric with a love for writing that even two years of freelance editing couldn't quash. She began taking poetry seriously after reading at Karen Hogan's Saturday Salons in 2003. Ryan organized, edited, and published the 2005 *Teen Soup Anthology* with the help of WingSpan Press.

Tania Selden — Tania Selden recently started attending Saturday Salons. This is the first time her works have appeared in *Livermore Wine Country Literary Harvest*.

Selene Steese — Selene Steese is a prolific writer who loves to perform her work. She teaches writing workshops throughout the Bay Area, and immerses herself in words as much as possible. "It sometimes seems," she says, "as though I tumbled out of the womb with a pen in my hand."

Frank Thornburgh — Grew up in rural Indiana, California Police Officer, Physics/Math Degree, OL-5 Greenland Engineer, New Jersey Fireman, Special Forces Reserves + others over 44 years, Parachutist and Marksmanship Instructor U.S. Army, N.B.C. Instructor Army Reserve, Substitute teacher, Purchaser and re-builder of 15 residential homes, Writing short articles for magazines and newspapers

Charan Sue Wollard — Charan Sue Wollard has lived in the beautiful Livermore Valley over 30 years. She is a poet, storyteller, editor, painter and student of metaphysics. In her day job, she helps people she likes buy and sell homes. Her writing has appeared in the *Carquinez Review*, *SV* magazine and other publications.

Steve Workman — Steve Workman has written several short stories that have been published in various anthologies over the past four years. All of the stories are related in some way and will be incorporated into a larger work of fiction once the final story is written.

Proofreaders

Sue Padgett — Sue has lived in the Tri-Valley most of her life. When the compliance officer is not at work, she enjoys spending time with her husband Fred and Rummy, their miniature Schnauzer who believes he is a giant. Cycling, photography, writing and editing are among her favorite pursuits.

Index of Authors

Author	Page	Title
Armknecht, Ian Ray	49	(Untitled)
	130	(Familiarity)
Blair, J.D.	46	Whitcomb's Trill
	153	Empties
Carey, Diana	106	Purple Orchids
	152	Hangnails,
Collins, David	10	The Best Sports Play I Ever Saw Involved a Trombone
	94	Monoblogue
Coyle, Pat	126	Robert Bly Changed my Life
Darter, Tom	44	Sweetman
	51	Genre Nano Fiction
	132	Fatherhood
	174	Voice Voyage
Gower, Harold	98	Adam
	105	Frank Rothman
Hambrecht, Jason	50	Nano Non-Fiction
Hardiman, David	52	Not Really Kafka, Just Kafka-esque
	164	Last Revolutionary War Widow Dies
Hoex, Bryant	24	Midnight in Texas
Hogan, Karen	1	A Story is Meant to be Passed Around
	139	A Peach Cobbler Tale
	176	The Unnanounced Visitor
Jones, Ben	63	The Cow and the Mountain Lion
kay, sandra	43	ego at large (again!)
	82	blogspot
	162	caught up (9 of 12)
Kinkead Bobbie	67	Saving the Woods

Author	Page	Title
Lock, Jennifer	78	Mary and the Divine one
	136	Sunday
	144	Government Cheerios
Mayall, Susan	21	The Day the Ice Cream Disappeared
	80	Lunch With Kitty
Mays, Ethel	61	Comin' Down the Hill
	70	When Rocks Offer Comfort
	147	Thunderheads
Mima, Kathy	112	The Journal
	146	Before Smog
	163	Speed of Life
Patton, Cynthia	37	Halloween Hair
Pollard, Kelly	71	Irish Twins
Rien, Timothy B.	12	Too Long Between Something and Nothing
Ryan, Grace	131	My Rightful Father
	151	Another Rain Pom
	173	Saturday Evening in Harvard Square
Selden, Tania	135	Amber Afternoon
	138	My Parents' Bedroom
Steese, Selene	8	Why I Write Part I
	110	Why I Write Part II
	167	The Chair
	177	Why I Write Part III
Thornburgh, Frank	59	Puberty Problems
	99	Andy
Wollard, Charan Sue	134	My Daughter's Wedding
	172	Creature from the Black Lagoon
Workman, Steve	117	The Picture

4TH STREET STUDIO

Livermore's Literary Arts Center — Where Something Happens so Something Else Can Happen

Presents

Saturday Salons
at 4th Street Studio
Livermore's Literary Arts Center
Third Saturday of every month

2235 4th Street — Livermore
7:30 PM
Call 925.456.3100
or email
4thstreetstudio@pacbell.net
for more information

"There is a there, there!" said Gertrude, raising her stein

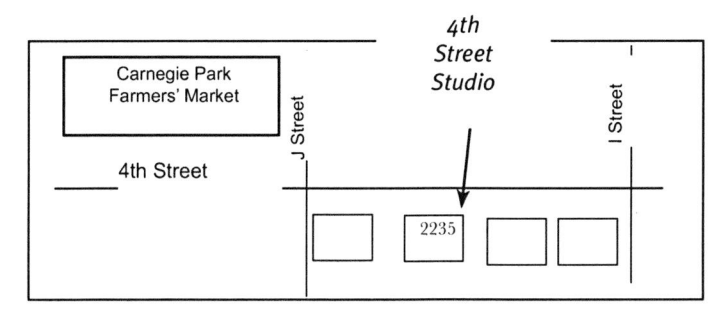